# The Ides

## An Extraordinary Affair of AJ Raffles & Sherlock Holmes

## Penny Doyle Douglas

Icehouse Publishing

*Chapter One*

At half-past twelve, Bunny Manders was running for his life. Thinking so quick it was not even a thought, he skidded between two cabs standing in a line awaiting the emergence of gentlemen from the clubs along that street after their late suppers, to carry them on to cards rooms and cigar lounges. He willed his feet to be light, to dampen the sound of shoes never meant for speed, and dropped into the shadow of a hulking, cheap-looking hansom, ducking low to be sure he would not be seen. To his relief, the two raging beasts in evening dress who had been tailing him jogged right past without noticing him. After a dozen panting breaths, the echoes of their angry voices had faded, and he cautiously stepped out into the muzzy light cast by gas lamps and cab's lanterns.

He'd left his coat behind, and thought he might just be able to dash back and fetch it. He nudged a sleeping driver, who snorted and opened his eyes but did not much adjust his posture. Bunny pulled out his billfold from inside his jacket, flashed its contents at the driver and implored him to wait. The driver agreed at once, even sat upright and addressed the horses to prove his worth. Bunny tossed the billfold into the open window of the cab, heard it thud, then fall to the floor.

As he rounded the back of the cab, he lost his luck and his earlier pursuers appeared out of the darkness. Each took him by an arm, and they marched him into an alley.

"You know those cheques you wrote us are worthless, Manders," one growled. They'd gambled together, and though Bunny had been up nearly forty early in the game, by the end he was down over two hundred. Unwilling to part with the very last of his cash—now safe on the floor of the cab—he had written each of his creditors a cheque, despite well-knowing he was already overdrawn at his bank.

"Whyever would you th-think—?" Bunny stammered; the shorter of the two was also the more athletic, and he had a firm grip on Bunny's lapels.

"Soon's he came in from the gents', Vandenberg had a great laugh, telling us he's sure you must be down to your last pennies, the way you spend. Says you're cut off from the family money."

"Not cut off!" Bunny protested, forgetting his terror in a moment of true indignation. Cut off, indeed!

"We want the money you owe, in notes if you

please, and we want it immediately."

"I haven't got any cash, I swear! Check my pockets; I've nothing." The two gamblers felt his pockets, even turned out one in his trousers. "You see? I only carry cheques after dark. It's too risky to walk the streets with cash, you gents know how dangerous London can be!"

For a moment the two looked as if they might accept his pleas, but after a quick exchange of glances, the one not already holding his lapels reared back a fist. There was a crash of pain and a high, shrieking sound, and then Bunny was being shaken awake on the floor of his cab.

Staring down at him was a moon-pale, smirk-smiling face, something confusingly familiar about the way his dark hair curled above his smooth forehead.

"Weak jaw, my boy," said he. "Honestly, they hardly touched you."

In a rush, his evening's exploits came back to him, and Bunny reached without any pause for caution into the inner pocket of his jacket, but found it empty. "I believe you may have something that belongs to me," he said, trying to sound more lucid than he felt. He got up onto his knee, then onto the edge of the hard wooden seat of the cab.

His antagonist adjusted slightly the angle of his smirk as he replied, "Then I suppose perhaps we have something to talk about." He produced a silver cigarette case, opened it, and extended it toward Bunny, who shook his head in the negative. The man removed one for himself, and set it between his lips while he went through the motions of striking a match and lighting it. "Must be quite a story," he mused, "Those two were in no joking mood, clearly. And you were afraid—I can see you're afraid even now."

Bunny said nothing, though he did lift his chin a bit.

The man held the cigarette between his first two fingers, cradling Bunny's billfold so as to dip in the fingers of his other hand to examine the contents. "You've a hundred pounds in here! Where were you off to in such a hurry you'd toss it into a cab like you did?" His tone was pure amusement, and Bunny felt he was being made the butt of a joke.

"My business is my own," he said hotly.

"My dear fellow," the man said, and leaned up and forward, crowding Bunny in the slight space of the cab. "It seems you misapprehend the current situation. By putting this wallet into my hands —however unintentional the act may have been— you have made me a partner in your business." The billfold was cupped loosely in his hand, and Bunny made a grab for it, but the curly-haired man whisked it back beside his own ear, slouching easily in his seat. In that moment of arrogant ease—with the angled glow of the lantern light cutting across the man's face—Bunny suddenly knew him.

"Raffles!" he said. "Do you remember me?"

The man straightened slightly. "Remind me," he prompted, examining Bunny's face more closely, with something like suspicion.

"I fagged for you at school," Bunny prompted, thinking AJ Raffles ought to remember him, at least a little, as it was he who had bestowed the rabbit-y label upon him.

Raffles' eyes narrowed significantly, but at once he burst out, "Bunny! Is it really you?"

"Yes! Yes, it's me," Bunny replied with enthusiasm. "What a lucky thing, to toss my billfold into a cab at random and find it's an old friend inside." Bunny fully expected that now they were reacquainted as grown-up former schoolmates, Raffles would hand over his hundred with all speed.

Raffles, cigarette held somehow elegantly between his teeth, leaned away and clapped his hands together, a visible ripple of amusement shivering through him. "Well, Bunny Manders, what a small, small world," he grinned. "Of course—of course I remember you! The great rabbit himself. Oh, what a sad turn that we meet amidst your current difficulties. But didn't I hear you had some significant inheritance?"

Bunny collapsed backward on the bench seat,

feeling his defeats stacking up one upon the other, on top of his chest. "I've spent it all," he admitted gloomily. He went on to explain he'd been the only child and inherited well, but now found himself relieved his parents were no longer alive to witness his shame. Raffles quickly countered with suggestions—hadn't Bunny written verse for the school mag? Had he a flat full of furniture he could sell off? —but it was all noise to Bunny, who had already discovered the literary life was not one that paid, and whose every stick of furniture was already at the mercy of the pawnbroker. He had been in debt before the night's gambling binge; now he was in irretrievable ruins. The more Raffles inquired, the deeper into despair Bunny sank.

In a fit of hopelessness, Bunny made to climb down from the cab, reaching for the door, but Raffles blocked his way. "What's your hurry?" he demanded, his expression an inscrutable blend of anxiety and amusement.

"Let me pass," Bunny blurted.

Raffles narrowed his eyes with a sort of knowing suspicion.

"Tell me first where you are going."

In a hot instant, Bunny withdrew a pistol from his pocket and touched it to his own forehead. Expecting shock or even terror in Raffles' expression, Bunny saw neither; instead he looked impressed—even seemed to anticipate whatever might follow with some strange pleasure. Bunny lowered the pistol.

"Damn me to hell," he muttered as he did so. "And you, you villain," he fired at Raffles. "I believe you wished for me to pull the trigger."

Raffles gave a small shake of his head, and flicked the smouldering butt-end of his cigarette through the open window onto the pavement.

"Never have I been so enthralled. I wouldn't have imagined such a bold notion from you, Bunny! No I have not other choice but to keep you close at hand." Raffles' expression had turned to one of thoughtful concern, as if he were plotting some scheme. He warned, "But don't stage such a stunt again; I have no patience for a pantomime. Between the two of us we can think a way out of your crisis." He hummed, and then almost as if he had just been reminded of it, he added, "Only first, give over the gun."

Bunny realized Raffles was going to help him after all, and the wash of relief he felt nearly drowned him. He handed over the pistol. Raffles thumped on the ceiling of the cab and shouted to the driver.

It was not a long drive to Raffles' rooms at the Albany, and along the way he said little, smoking another cigarette, and looking contemplative. Bunny stole glances at him at intervals, marveling at how little he had changed since their school days—his curly dark hair still constantly on the verge of going wild, eyes full of curiosity, with his straight sloping nose and firm chin—and teased by the intensity of his own feelings for AJ Raffles returning in a flash. Admiring of him, certainly—nearly to the point of awe—and fond of his wit. But there were other, deeper feelings Bunny had harboured then, for the accomplished cricketer and in-demand pal, and they flickered to life again—like setting the match to a candle wick—and Bunny wondered what else Raffles may remember of him.

Raffles' rooms were comfortable, neither extravagant nor meagre. They'd detoured for Bunny to reclaim his overcoat from the cards room, and so he followed Raffles' lead and hung it on a peg inside the door. Leading the way into the sitting room, Raffles offered to pour them whisky and water, which Bunny gratefully accepted, given that his nerves were frayed to bits after his night of operatic turns—both emotional and physical. Bunny took an offered seat on a small sofa and Raffles settled on the edge of the fire, which was cold.

"Here's something I've never done before," Raffles mused, and before Bunny could ask to what he referred, Raffles reached inside his jacket, pulled forth Bunny's billfold, and tossed it to him. Bunny's relief surely showed on his face, and he tucked the wallet away immediately, not indulging an urge to look inside, lest Raffles feel affronted Bunny didn't trust him not to have robbed it.

"You'd better get some sleep, Bunny my boy," Raffles said, quick-draining his whisky. Bunny had only yet downed two swallows of his own. "I've a plan to get you set back to rights—something I was going to do anyway, but I won't mind some company. Not at all." He quirked up one side of his mouth, looking considerate. "But we've a long way to go."

"Oh? Where are we headed?" Bunny inquired, a light thrill burbling through him at the thought of joining AJ Raffles on a sojourn—one which might somehow re-fill Bunny's accounts, all the better.

"Wherever the ten a.m. train is headed," Raffles said curtly, and already he was making moves toward his bedroom. "Honestly, what I've in mind can happen almost anywhere."

Bunny felt unsteady, but enticed by the promise of adventure. He smoothed his fine hair, more for something to busy his hand than for another purpose. "Well, I've got at least enough money to keep us going for a while," he suggested. "I admit I'd enjoy the company."

Since the sofa was quite short, Raffles suggested they share the bed—undoubtedly after the evening he'd had, Bunny must sleep heavily and shouldn't be bothered if Raffles happened to snore. They both laughed at the self-deprecating joke, and Bunny toed off his shoes, untrussed himself from his evening suit, down to his trousers and under-vest. Raffles emerged from a small dressing room between his bedroom and the bath wearing a nightshirt and a very fine dressing gown of smooth, emerald satin. Bunny averted his eyes, stretched out on top of the coverlet with his ankles crossed and his hands balled up together on his belly, taking up as little space as possible.

Raffles doused the light and Bunny could just make out his silhouette, black on grey, as he removed his robe and hung it on the post at the foot of the bed, then pulled back the blankets and slipped beneath them. The dark seemed to want whispering, and Raffles said in a low voice, "Not cold, then, Bunny?"

Bunny shrugged, and while surely Raffles could not see it, there was a rustle of his undershirt against the coverlet and a shifting of the down-filled pillow beneath his head.

"You will be," Raffles said, quiet but crisp. "Cover up."

Bunny did as he was told, stepping out of the bed, then back in once he'd shifted the covers.

"Good night, Raffles," he said, laying on his back though it was not his preferred sleeping position. He knew sleep was a long way off, if it would come at all.

"Night, Bunny," Raffles said through a yawn, then fell quiet. Bunny's eyes had adjusted to the dark, but even still he could only make out a slit of street-glow between the window curtains, and some distant light from elsewhere in the apartment oozed in beneath the door. He could make out the bedposts, and there was an oval mirror hung on the wall beside the wardrobe which seemed to glow rather than reflect. Otherwise, there was nothing to see. He thought he might count sheep.

He wondered if Raffles remembered at all, as Bunny vividly did, a night long ago when In the waning hours of a night-long celebration of Raffles' heroic showing in a championship cricket match, Raffles had cornered him, pressed close to him, and kissed him. Raffles' mouth had smelled of cherry brandy, but he was steady, and though they never talked of it again, Bunny had felt in the instant nothing predatory or exploitive—as was all too common among the boys at their school—but rather something passionate, affectionate. Whenever he had occasion to re-member it, Bunny felt a melancholy longing that was the self-same emotion he'd had at the time; it came on as sharp and anguished years later as it had that drunken night. Bunny rearranged his prayer-folded hands so that he could pinch his forearms, a distraction if not truly a penance.

Before he could fully resettle, Raffles grasped him by the wrist and pulled Bunny's hand to his chest, and then to his lips. He lay a soft, dry kiss against the lowest knuckles, then dragged his chin, lips, and nose across the back of Bunny's slack hand. Bunny did not resist, did not withdraw; he was waiting to see what might happen next, as if he were watching a stage play. But what a play that would be! He smiled at the thought, but kept still. Raffles, trailing whispers of kisses along the length of Bunny's fingers, and then against his palm, shifted his body closer, though still they only touched at the points where Raffles' lips brushed Bunny's hand and wrist. Bunny drew in a full breath, and quietly sighed it away.

As Bunny's elbow was bent, his hand in Raffles' hand there by his chest, it was not so far to go that soon Raffles lay impotent kisses against the fine cotton of Bunny's small clothes, upon the tip of his shoulder. The shock of his half-wet lips when they touched Bunny's throat made Bunny inhale harshly, and Raffles drew back just so that Bunny could still feel the cool exhalations drying the damp spot of his kiss. Having no desire to discourage him, Bunny let go his breath softly, and brushed the backs of his fingers against Raffles' jaw. Another rearrangement, slow and quiet, and Raffles leant up on his elbow; Bunny could sense more than see his face hovering above. He reached for Raffles' shoulder and rested his hand there, neither pushing nor pulling, but Raffles read the message in it, and in a moment his mouth found Bunny's, and Bunny parted his lips so they might find their places.

The kisses were wonderful—lips parted, tongue-tips teasing—and Bunny's body warmed from crown to toes, though he stayed still and soft through it all, not wanting to seem overeager. Somehow, even with Raffles kissing him, and holding his face, and then sliding his hand down Bunny's chest and gripping his side, Bunny worried he was mistaking the intention. He'd no wish to put them both at risk of arrest—of ruin—by pressing too far beyond the proper boundaries. All this he thought even with his mouth open and Raffles' tongue wandering about inside it.

Bunny had nearly forgotten his hand, still on Raffles' shoulder, and suddenly remembered it, so moved it, stroking down Raffles' back until his hand met the edge of the blankets. Despite the fact both men were dressed, Bunny felt too endangered to let his hands wander beneath the covers, so reversed course until he felt the skin of Raffles' neck, and then the slick softness of his hair. Raffles seemed to have no such hesitation about beneath-the-bedclothes activity; the heat of their kisses was growing, both of them becoming breathless even in their near-silence, and Raffles slid his hand over Bunny's chest in a most intimate manner, feeling for the shape of him, purposely brushing his thumb hard against the nub of Bunny's nipple, which tightened in response. Bunny's fingers wound up in the curls of Raffles' hair, and held him in place. Greedy kisses brought them both to huffing —humming—and Raffles stroked a firm hand into the crease of Bunny's hip, then up to the fastenings of his trousers. He broke away.

Even his whisper was loud in the quiet of the room. "Yes or no, Bunny?" he asked, almost gently, though his panting breath gave him away as roiling in the same tumultuous state he had incited in Bunny. A silent moment passed, stretching out between them. Their chests beat against each other, both men breathing hard. Raffles dipped down for a quick kiss, sucking Bunny's lower lip and pulling away. His hand stayed still at the front of Bunny's waist as he waited for Bunny's response.

"I think," Bunny murmured, ". . .no."

Raffles said nothing, and as he drew away, his hand moved up Bunny's chest, making motions almost as if he were buttoning him up. He patted Bunny three times, over his heart, then rolled away to give Bunny his back.

# Chapter Two

I n the light of day, nothing was said about the previous night's intimate exchange; Bunny imagined Raffles' pride might be hurt, so despite a small wish to explain the rejection as the product of Bunny's fear of committing a crime rather than of a true lack of feeling, he kept mum. They dressed, had tea and buns enough to qualify as breakfast, and as Raffles had suggested, boarded a midmorning train headed northeast.

As the train slowed ten minutes from Norwood, Bunny stood to gaze out the window of their shared compartment. Raffles leaned close against his back, perhaps only to secure a clear view, though Bunny could not be certain. Thus far in their reacquaintance, feeling certain had not been a luxury afforded to Bunny—about anything.

"My good man, I hope you are feeling a sense of adventure," Raffles said, turning back inward to put away the cigarette case he'd been holding, and to gather his overcoat and umbrella. "I'm afraid we must take advantage of the moment, and jump."

"Jump!" Bunny exclaimed. "From a moving train?"

"For reasons I haven't time to explain, I have reason to believe showing my face at the station would endanger us both. Come now, we're at a crawl, this is our chance."

Bunny felt a panicky fluster, but shrugged quickly into his own coat and followed Raffles out of their compartment, to the end of the carriage. It was true the train was taking a large curve at very low speed, but Bunny had terrifying visions of broken ankles—or worse—and turned wide eyes on Raffles, whose smile was as charming as ever it had been, his eyes glinting a sort of giddiness. He tilted his head toward the opening where he had slid the door aside. "Easy as falling off a log," he reassured.

"It's not a log I'm worried about falling off!" Bunny cried, "Or falling under."

"Just watch."

Raffles took two long strides and was off, checking his balance as he landed. He waved furiously to urge Bunny on, jogging along beside the open door.

"Now, Bunny! Now or never!"

Bunny steeled his courage with a deep breath, and tried to copy Raffles' easy jump to the passing ground. He stumbled forward a few steps, the weight of his own chest nearly pitching him head over heels, but Raffles caught him in a sturdy embrace around his back, then thumped his shoulder.

"Well done! I'd say you're a natural."

Exhilarated by his success—feats of physical prowess had never been his specialty—Bunny felt a smile break across his face, and the two began to walk; it wasn't long before they came to a road, and soon enough a shabby looking old fellow passed by driving a donkey, his wagon full of sheared wool.

"I say," Raffles halloed, "I wonder if we might trouble you for a ride? Damned if we aren't as lost as two lambs—we left our hotel for the station and must have gotten turned around." His lie was so smooth Bunny nearly believed it.

The farmer looked skeptical until Raffles added, "We can pay you, of course," and named an exorbitant sum equal to the coins in Bunny's pocket. Another of Raffles' charming grins, and the two were welcomed onto the bench of the wagon and promised to be delivered to the village.

"What village are we coming to, by the way?" Raffles asked as the driver whipped the donkey and they started to jostle onward.

"Sheepmeadow," replied the driver. "Nice little village."

Raffles glowed an expression of sheer delight. "Sheepmeadow," he repeated. "Why, that does sound absolutely lovely." Bunny longed to demand explanations from Raffles, but didn't dare question him in front of a stranger. He was in for a penny, though, and so clearly he must be in for a pound. Whatever Raffles' scheme to help Bunny cover his debts, Bunny needed him, and would go along.

In a tavern called Button's, the only such place in the village of Sheepmeadow, consulting detective Sherlock Holmes was sat one of a pair of armchairs by the fireplace, across from his porcine elder brother Mycroft. The younger Holmes, smoking a cigarette, had the previous day saved an innocent man from facing trial on charges of a murder that neither he nor anyone had committed, as the victim was engaged in a scheme to fake his own demise. Before he could resume the comfort of his rooms at Baker Street in London, however, his brother had arrived quite unexpectedly, with a request that Sherlock use his intelligence and discretion to aid in the recovery of sensitive documents, which were accompanied on their travels from the colonies by a sizable quantity of rubies and diamonds. The elder Holmes held an unofficial government post which made him the fulcrum of a rather delicate lever, which he wished to weigh heavily in the English favour by intercepting the secret papers; the jewels were of no interest to him.

In the moment, however, the two Holmes men were engaged in a conversation of a more personal nature. Mycroft settled his teacup in its saucer and lowered it near the arm of his chair. "You should count yourself lucky, brother, not to have the burden of a paramour."

"Oh, indeed?" Sherlock prompted, sensing his brother had broached the subject more for the opportunity to gloat than to in any manner comfort Sherlock.

"I've sent three notes to Lady Tinsley in as many days and have yet to receive a reply. There is some amusement in the pursuit, but ultimately the frustration of the whole affair makes one doubt whether it is a worthy use of one's time."

Sherlock only lifted his eyebrows and gave a mild shrug. Romantic pursuits were note remotely his area of expertise.

"At any rate," Mycroft finished, "I envy you the freedom to concentrate wholly on intellectual pursuits. *Affaires de coeur* amount to not much more than a heap of woes."

By the time Mycroft had finished speaking, Sherlock was less than half-listening, though, as the vaguely familiar figure of a man had taken up a seat nearby. The newcomer had a tightly folded copy of the morning newspaper in one hand, but Sherlock could see rather plainly that he was not reading, but rather looking at Sherlock, with the paper as a useful prop. Nonetheless Sherlock had caught the man's gaze twice, and each time the man had dropped his eyes to the paper.

Mycroft squinted at Sherlock, having caught on

to his distraction. In a low voice, he prompted, "You see something of interest?"

"Not something," Sherlock replied. "Someone. And I am not so much interested as unsettled. Look in the glass above the fire; can you see the man in the navy suit, over your right shoulder? With the newspaper."

Mycroft glanced up, then back at his brother. "The one with the scar across his nose? A rough looking fellow to be sure, but I thought by now you were used to being espied on by all sorts. If anything, he is only doing reconnaissance on you; I see no sign that he is armed." Mycroft's ability to size up a stranger was even more developed than Sherlock's, so the younger Holmes was persuaded by his assertion. Sherlock pursed his lips, ill-at-ease to know he was being watched, even if not threatened with immediate harm. Mycroft's noisome smirk returned. "Or perhaps it is only that he enjoys looking at you."

Sherlock huffed irritation through his nostrils. "My skin is crawling," he said.

Mycroft dismissed the matter with his usual crisp efficiency. "I count him out as harmless."

Once Raffles and Bunny had alighted from the wagon and handed the farmer the promised over-payment, they took stock of the small row of shops, post office, and bank that constituted the village center. "These little villages are all so similar to one another, Bunny; we could be anywhere."

"Well, this one's got a tavern, at least," Bunny countered, gesturing across the road. "And I'm a bit hungry. What say you, Raffles?"

Raffles agreed and they made their way to the public house, where they were seated at a small, round table just on the edge of the cigar room, with a view of the fire. Two men sat nearby, in armchairs. One was tall, slim, and elegant; the other sturdy, mustachioed, and still.

"I told you before I prefer you not involve her, Holmes," said the stocky gentleman with a frown bordering on a scowl.

"True enough, you did. And as I offered before, in Miss Adler's defense," the taller man retorted, "She is bright and fearless, and much as we might prefer it otherwise, there are places in society not open to men into which the infiltration of a woman like Irene Adler can be invaluable. In short, Watson: much as you may disapprove, we need her."

The two fell into silence, and the man called Watson stood up from his armchair and began to pace the room. Raffles and Bunny asked for the chop and ale, and sat awaiting its arrival. Bunny could not help notice that Raffles' gaze was unguardedly fixed upon the profile of the other man, Holmes. Watson approached them, speaking chummily.

"Down from London, you gents?" he ventured. "Same as my friend and me."

"What makes you think so?" Raffles replied, barely glancing at Watson, who stood by with hands clasped behind his back.

"Until you arrived, we were the only two people I've seen who weren't dressed for labour or service. I'd say your cravat gave you away." He turned toward Bunny, "And you, your shoes."

"Well, now, that's a fine trick!" Bunny enthused. Raffles sniffed but said nothing. "I'd say that's rather sharp of Mr— ah...?"

"Doctor John Watson," said the man, and offered them handshakes. "My friend, the detective Sherlock Holmes."

Holmes joined them, and they exchanged greetings.

"Policeman?" Raffles asked.

"Certainly not," Holmes replied. "The police consult me when they've gone wrong. Which is more frequently than most upright citizens would prefer, I assure you."

"Is that right?" Raffles mused, and he fixed Holmes with a curious stare. "Now, didn't I read about you in the papers? Something about a girl's stolen inheritance. Yes! Yes, I'm sure of it!"

Holmes smiled, but lowered his eyes. Bunny felt something akin to alarm.

"Well, how charming to meet such an esteemed gentleman," Raffles gushed, and reached to shake Holmes' hand once more. They held the clinch longer than strictly necessary, as far as Bunny was concerned.

"He's Raffles," Bunny blurted. "AJ Raffles, the cricketer. He's in the newspapers, too." Their new friends looked appropriately impressed, though Raffles made a motion with his hand to wave off Bunny's accolades. "Well. Not now, it's not the season for cricket. But he's very well known!"

Raffles grinned but deflected by saying, "My friend, Bunny Manders."

"Perhaps we four city gentlemen might share a whisky, since we're all fish out of water together here," Raffles suggested, looking only at Holmes. The four agreed without committing to an appointment time, and Holmes and Watson excused themselves and bid their goodbyes.

They were served their meals and Bunny jabbed his cutlery viciously. To his lamb and potatoes he muttered, "Having too many friends has the strange effect of draining one's accounts, you know."

Raffles shrugged, unbothered by Bunny's likely

too-obvious jealousy at his flirtatious manner with the detective, Mr Holmes. "I've no intention to spend a penny," he assured, though Bunny couldn't begin to guess what he had in mind, and he was too irked, just then, to ask.

Bunny noticed at a table against the opposite wall a slender, tall woman with a fine-featured face. There was a pot of tea on her table, and her gloves, and she was reading a book which appeared to be something handwritten like a diary rather than a novel or reference. Just as Bunny was about to turn his attention back to Raffles, despite not yet having formulated words appropriate to the force of his feeling, the woman looked up at Bunny, and smiled. She held his gaze so boldly, and was so mischievously pretty, Bunny could not but stare back, and eventually, when his shock subsided, return the smile. The woman folded her book shut and lay it on the table, arranging her gloves atop it, all the while maintaining the look she shared with Bunny, and at length she raised a finger and beckoned him.

"You must excuse me, Raffles," Bunny said quickly, and swiped at the corners of his mouth with his serviette before dropping it onto his plate. "There's a lady there I think requires my assistance." Raffles looked surprised, and searched the room until he found the woman in question, but raised no protest, only hummed acquiescence as Bunny crossed the room.

∞∞∞

Sherlock Holmes had bid goodbye to his friend Dr Watson, and discharged him as his proxy to a meeting with local police, who bored and annoyed Holmes beyond measure. He had resumed the arm-chair by the fire, which he had come to think of as his own, at least for as long as he was trapped in the village of Sheepmeadow. It had a wide view of the room, into and out of which passed many people—a few of them even interesting—and another angle allowed him to surveille passersby through a sizable window to the street. The well-dressed supposed cricketer (Holmes did not follow sport, and with the exceptions of some younger years spent boxing and fencing, neither engaged in any), AJ Raffles approached and asked if he might take the chair nearby, where earlier had sat John Watson, and the prior evening, Holmes' brother Mycroft.

"Perhaps you enjoy a Sullivan?" Raffles asked, holding out his open cigarette case.

Holmes demurred, "I prefer my pipe, but I thank you."

"I think you may have missed a spot," Raffles said then, and Holmes shot him a puzzled, questioning look. Gesturing in the direction of Holmes' knee, Raffles clarified. "The way you're swiping at your trousers, I thought you must be trying to remove some telltale stain."

Sure enough, Holmes found he had been mindlessly circling his fingertips against his knee, one of many little tics that emerged when he was deep in consideration about a case. He stopped, instead folding his hands together at his waist. As he looked away from his own hands, he caught sight of the same scarred, surly character he'd spotted the previous night, just then ensconced at the far side of the room and hardly subtle about watching Holmes.

Raffles must have noticed, for he turned to look half-over his shoulder in the direction of Holmes' gaze, and given the observer was utterly alone, saw the man with the scarred face. "Pal of yours?" Raffles asked, and the implication was clear to anyone in the know, as Holmes was.

"Certainly not," Holmes frowned. "Though by appearing here just now, he's removed any doubt that he is spying upon my visit to this village, though the purpose for it as yet eludes me."

Raffles flashed the warm, charming smile once more, and the way he looked Holmes deeply in the eyes left him feeling oddly shaken. "I can imagine his reason is quite similar to my own," Raffles ventured. Holmes averted his eyes and felt his ears warming, pursed his lips against an involuntary, mostly unwelcome smile. Raffles offered a non sequitur. "I'd bet my last you've got a beautifully cut evening suit, blue-grey to bring out the positively astonishing colour of your eyes. I'd wager you dress your lapel with a handsome buttonhole—perhaps a green carnation?"

Holmes at last looked again at Raffles's smooth, earnest face, to make double-sure there was no misunderstanding between them. Raffles' expression assured him he was reading the situation correctly. He lifted his eyebrows.

"Put on that suit tonight, and we'll go for a walk. Perhaps find some entertainment, for two bored city fellows?" He looked expectant in a manner that did not welcome—nor even expect—rebuff.

"All right," Holmes agreed. "A walk would be quite pleasant."

"Shall I meet you here? Eight o'clock?" Raffles offered, looking like the proverbial cat who'd got the best of his matron's canary.

Holmes agreed to the time of a rendezvous and excused himself, offering a handshake which Raffles accepted with a gentleness which made Holmes feel as if his hand had been kissed rather than clasped.

Raffles looked around for Bunny, and spotted him still seated with the woman who had earlier beckoned him, at a table small enough that her chair did not need to be slid closer to Bunny's, though it was obvious that was precisely what had occurred. The woman's cheeks and lips were pinched-pink and she did not miss a chance to touch Bunny's coatsleeve as they chatted. Bunny looked, if not besotted, at least intrigued, and why not? The woman was quite pretty. But Raffles could scent in the air what she was about, and it was not innocent romance. He'd seen her sort of dress before, with telltale stitching where pockets were hidden, and she wore a locket which almost certainly held the hair of her dear, dead father or guardian uncle, who had meant to leave her a fortune, but who had been cruelly tricked by a young nurse or a butler. Or so the story might go; confidence artists had many a compelling tale, but all for the same purpose.

"Bunny," Raffles began, but before he could press upon his friend the urgency with which they must leave, Bunny cut him off.

All blitheness and naivete, Bunny introduced them. "Miss Irene Adler. She works with Sherlock Holmes, Raffles! He's ever-so-dependent on her for her—" he mugged in a manner that brought Raffles almost physical pain, "*feminine intuition.*"

"Yes, lovely to meet you, I'm sure," Raffles said quickly. He fixed her with an expression of obviously false friendliness and said through a smile, "There's no profit to be made here, Miss Adler."

Bunny looked stupefied; Miss Adler looked grim. Raffles scolded her, "He's barely out of his boyhood." Before either Bunny or Miss Adler could voice a protest, he commanded, "Go and settle our bill, won't you Bunny?" Appearing to yield to Raffles' wisdom, or perhaps merely remembering Raffles had promised to find Bunny enough money to settle his debts before he lost his life over them, Bunny did as he was told. Miss Adler scowled at him.

"You've got an eye as keen as razors, sir," she said coolly. "Perhaps Sherlock Holmes could find some use for you, as well."

With a triumphant smirk, Raffles told her, "I certainly hope he does *find a use for me*. Good day, my dear lady."

# Chapter Three

That evening, Holmes and Watson had their supper together at the tavern, happily un-molested by the lurker Holmes had spotted twice in as many visits. "What say you to a few hands of cards, Holmes?" Watson asked, dabbing at his mustache with his serviette between mouthfuls of mutton stew.

"I'm afraid I must decline the invitation, my dear fellow." Holmes repressed a smile, tilting his head down.

"Oh? I hope you haven't made arrangements with Miss Adler. An unmarried woman might get ideas about a man spending time with her after dark, you know."

"No, no," Holmes assured him in a light tone. "Not at all. It's only Mr Raffles, who we met at lunch-time, has asked me to accompany him on a tour of the village center. Perhaps to find some amusement, but if not, at least to further our new acquaintance."

Watson, who had looked pleased when Holmes

denied a plan to meet Miss Adler, frowned upon hearing he instead meant to walk out with AJ Raffles.

"Ah, Holmes," he said, in a reticent tone. "Do you not think Raffles a bit of a ruffian? His name only seems to appear in the society pages in reference to tawdry rumours, or when no names are given in the case of a true scandal, there's a whiff of him off it."

Holmes' interest was further enlivened by this observation. "Is that so? I leave the reading of elite gossip to you, Watson, and look how you have intrigued me! I'm sure your intention was to warn me off of any association with him, but in reality you have dangled an irresistible bit of bait before me. Now I am more certain than ever that I must get to know Mr Raffles all the better!"

"Whatever for?" Watson was rattled, but looked on the verge of acquiescing to Holmes' arguments.

"A real gentleman who regularly is aligned with unsavoury behaviour interests me greatly, Watson. Where there are rumours and scandal, often there is crime. Perhaps Mr Raffles has information that may serve me, in future."

Watson sighed out surrender. "Suit yourself, Holmes. Only be on your guard, as ever."

"Your advice, as always, my dear fellow, is sound. And I shall follow it."

Bunny watched Raffles shave his face, a towel tucked into the neck of his shirt to protect it. They had taken space in a rooming house outside the village center, so as not to always be in the thick of things. Given Bunny's sorry situation, he could not argue against such a precaution, just in case one or more of his creditors may have somehow followed them to Sheepmeadow.

"There's something you should know, Bunny," Raffles said, tilting up his chin as he ran the blade down the side of his throat. "What you do with it once you know is your own decision, but I want there to be no misunderstandings between us."

"What's that, Raffles?" Bunny asked, sitting upright on the edge of the room's one wide but sagging bed.

"My interest in Sherlock Holmes is entirely professional," Raffles said firmly. Bunny felt a strange tingle of something like relief. The previous evening, when they had kissed and caressed each other in the dark of Raffles' bedroom, felt distant, and Bunny had no claim on Raffles—he'd even refused an advance he'd truly wished to accept—yet it seemed Raffles was intimating he had no romantic intention toward the famous detective, and Bunny was glad of it.

Raffles continued. "Sherlock Holmes, in a village like this, without a case to work on? I don't think so. The man is as famous for his burrowing down in Baker Street as he is for his skill at deductive reasoning. No, indeed, Bunny. I think Holmes is here on a case."

"Now you mention it, I have read about him that he is always reticent to leave London. But what professional interest do you have in Holmes' investigations, Raffles?" Bunny watched him as he toweled away stray corners of shave soap from under his ears and around the edge of his nose. He shook lavender scented after-shave into his palm, clapped his hands together, and patted the potion onto his face.

"I haven't been completely honest with you about how I intend to get your money," Raffles said haltingly. "The truth is I'm dreadfully hard up, and only pointed us toward Norwood on the basis of some rumours and a hunch."

Bunny was confounded. "You, Raffles? You, hard up?"

"Oh, yes. Just because I've rooms at the Albany, and play some cricket and belong to a few clubs, don't be fooled into thinking I'm well off. I'm in your same boat."

"Well, but what rumours?"

Raffles turned away from the cloudy, pitted mirror then, and soon began a slow circuit of the room, pacing. "There's a collection of jewels from the dark continent, sent as payment of some far greater debts, from a mine owner to our esteemed government. Rubies, mainly, but diamonds as well —great fat ones, all polished and cut and just waiting to be set into Her Majesty's newest coronet— and while they are bound for London, they appear to have wandered this way along their journey."

Bunny followed the story, but could not see how it might relate to him, or to Raffles. He waited, clutching the bed pillow across his middle so he'd something to hang onto.

"I think our friend Sherlock Holmes is here to find them, or to find who's caused this unexpected stop on their journey to London. And with a little charm and a lot of flattery, I think I may be able to get him to tell me what he knows."

A switch flipped in Bunny's mind, and he brightened. "Oh, brilliant! You'll get information from Holmes, then you can rescue the treasure and turn it over, and you'll be a hero! Surely there'll be a reward, and we can use it to shore ourselves up."

Raffles stopped pacing, and crossed his arms. He huffed a quick sigh and looked thoughtful. After a moment, a smile broke wide across his face. "Right you are, my dear fellow," he said. "It's a confidence game. No harm in it, though. If the information can be prised from Holmes, I say the race to claim the treasure is a fair game."

"It's very cunning, Raffles. I'd never have thought of it."

"No," Raffles said, quieter, and he stepped closer

to Bunny, who felt compelled to stand, putting them face to face, in striking distance. "No, I'm sure you wouldn't. You are all innocence and honesty, eh, Bunny?"

"Well," Bunny shrugged. "No. I don't just lose at cards—I cheat, too."

"I don't know I'd call it cheating if it doesn't help you win. You just play badly." Raffles smiled at his own joke. He was very close—too close, Bunny thought—but he was grateful for it, and didn't step backward. "I'd like to kiss you, again, Bunny," Raffles murmured, and his hand found Bunny's and gently clasped it. "Foolish of me to say so, I know—you've already rejected me once."

Bunny stepped forward and kissed him. He put his arms around Raffles' back, pinning his elbows to his sides, and Raffles was laughing at first, and said, "Bunny!" But quickly the embrace turned serious, and Raffles held Bunny at the waist, and pulled him close, and Bunny was too thrilled to even think of refusing Raffles again. They kissed and kissed, becoming breathless, and at last it was Raffles who pulled away. Bunny chased him, stealing a few kisses more, but Raffles held him steady and leaned back, his eyes searching Bunny's face.

"You remember once I kissed you?" he asked. "When we were at school."

"I've never forgotten it," Bunny told him. "I never will."

Raffles grinned, closed-lipped, then looked serious. "Going wrong with me means going all the way wrong, little rabbit. Are you certain you want to throw in with me?"

"With you? Raffles, it's like a dream!" Bunny couldn't keep the smile from his face. To be Raffles' friend was enticing, but to be much more than his friend—Bunny could think of nothing he wished for more. He'd wished for it for years.

"Another kiss, then," Raffles said, and slid one hand around to the small of Bunny's back, splayed fingers pressing in to claim him and pull him as near as they could be. "But just the one, or I'm sure to keep us both right here when I've an appointment to keep that could be the making of us."

Since Raffles was determined to keep to his meeting with Sherlock Holmes, Bunny insisted they leave their rented room, to pass the time. He thought being out in the world might distract him from thoughts of more embraces, more kisses, more. . .whatever more there may be. The two walked past the tavern to a billiards room with the name Robert & Sons painted in old, scratched, gold-and-black on the glass of its front door through which, inside a wood and glass booth, sat an ancient man with a chewed-up cigar between his teeth, and a gruff demeanour.

"Might I have change for a twenty?" Bunny

asked him. Raffles let out a low hum, over Bunny's shoulder. The old man near-shouted—perhaps he was deaf—in reply.

"How do you want that change for a twenty?"

Bunny told him, "A ten, two fives, four pound-notes, and the rest in coin, if you please."

Raffles turned his body so the billiards room was to his back. "Bunny..." he said, under his breath, but in what tone, Bunny could not precisely discern.

"There ya go," the old man shouted. "Ten. Five. Five. One, two, three, four. And coins."

"Thank you kindly," Bunny said, and swept up the coins into his hand, then into his trousers' pocket. The bills he counted and stacked and placed into his billfold. When he looked up again, he noticed that over Raffles' shoulder, a handful of working class young men had ceased their games and conversation, and were staring at Bunny and Raffles. He knew at once his mistake, and thought to turn and leave, but Raffles lead him in the opposite direction, to an unused table near the front window. He began to arrange the billiard balls for the start of a game. Bunny stood by, shifting his weight.

"Choose us some good sticks, my good man," Raffles prompted, his head tilting toward a nearby rack of cue sticks. As Bunny made a move toward it, four men from the next table moved closer to theirs, leaning on the table edge or on their upright sticks.

"Maybe we should place some bets, since you've got so much money," one of them said to Bunny, in the rough, unmistakable manner of bullies the world around.

"We are not gamblers, friend," Raffles said smoothly, "Perhaps you'd better move along."

Although the men continued glaring and staring, utterly flustering Bunny so that he lay hands on the first two sticks at hand and struggled to remove them from the rack, they did move along, not returning to their game, but gathering their overcoats and loose, half-smoked cigarettes, and leaving the hall.

The one who had spoken on their behalf, who Bunny thought must be the big man of the group, turned on his heel and smiled in a way that didn't match his words. "Dark out there. You gents should mind yourselves as you go."

Raffles only stared back at him, until the man turned away and went out the door.

Passing a stick to Raffles, Bunny said, "I don't like the implication."

"What's that, Bunny my boy?"

"That those men will be lurking about outside when we leave here."

Raffles gave Bunny a knowing, shrugging glance as he lined up a shot, and they began to play.

"In that case, what should we do, Raffles?"

Raffles motioned for Bunny to take his turn, and replied. "Well, I imagine that either we'll lose all our cash, and perhaps find ourselves murdered. Or we keep it, and get murdered nonetheless. No matter our approach, I think it's likely we end up with bashed-in heads." Bunny was shocked at the casual way Raffles offered his scenarios, both of which sent a chill shiver up the back of Bunny's neck.

"Surely we can avoid a fight?" he ventured, thinking they might find a back door to slip out of, or if they went on with their game long enough, the men might lose interest and move on before Raffles and Bunny left the billiards room.

Raffles sighed, and shrugged again. With resignation, he said, "This is just the way things are. Four of them, two of us. . ." he left the thought unfinished so that Bunny's mind turned over the odds of them finishing with their cash in hand, and their skulls intact.

One of the men came back in, then—not the aggressive, talky one who Bunny had taken for the leader, but one of his apparent toadies—and gruffed out, "We'll make yiz a deal. Hand over the billfold now, and you can leave outta here the same way you come in."

Bunny felt a rush of panic, but Raffles sounded cool and authoritative in his response. "But then we'd be skint, and that ain't how we came in." Bunny was impressed by his easy use of lower-class slang; even Raffles' accent was different, and his posture. Without thinking, Bunny felt for the wallet in his jacket, reassuring himself it was secure but probably giving the workman a fatal clue as to its location. Raffles made motions to leave, and Bunny wordlessly followed.

They started their walk to the rooming house, but it became evident very quickly that they were being followed by the small gang of toughs. "Follow close, Bunny," Raffles said authoritatively, beneath his breath. He ducked into an alley as they were passing it, and Bunny followed. Without speaking, Raffles motioned for Bunny to hide behind a stack of empty delivery crates, and he did, crouching in the shadows and trying to make himself small. Raffles hid across the alley, standing flat against a dark brick wall, partially concealed by a pile of scrap-wood.

Three of the men came into the alley—Bunny thought the fourth was probably on the lookout for police—and cast their gazes around. One of them held a knife in his left hand, the glint of the blade unmistakable in reflected light from a window high above them. In the evening half-dark, Bunny's eyes tricked him, making shadows into real men, and men into moving shadows. He wondered if the gang would be as easily fooled, and leave. He hunched his shoulders down even more, and leaned to his right.

All at once, Raffles sprang from his hiding place

and with the benefit of surprise, was able to land a sturdy blow with folded fist, straight in the middle of the knife-wielding tough's face. The man went down in a heap. A second man held a length of metal chain, which he flicked and swung, making Raffles dance out of his way.

"Now, Bunny!" Raffles shouted, using a length of the scrap-wood to block the swinging chain. Bunny bit down hard, sucked in a lungful of courage, and threw himself out from his hiding spot, tackling the third fellow—who so far appeared to be unarmed —to the ground so that he was face down in the packed dirt, and Bunny kept a knee firmly planted in his back. Raffles got hold of the other man's jacket and threw him against the stack of crates; the tough dropped his chain and made a clattering racket as he fell. Raffles delivered a series of punches to his face until he stopped fighting and lay limp on the ground.

Bunny's opponent had not surrendered to Bunny's knee at his back, had wriggled and pushed and fought his way free—he was much bigger than Bunny, in every measurement, and probably had a great deal more experience of fighting—and began to throw punches at him, which Bunny struggled to block. A jab to his ribs made him feel sick; a crack of knuckles just below his eye split the skin there and Bunny felt the hot rush of blood from the wound. The tough found his mate's discarded length of chain and bent to fetch it, but as he regained his feet,

Raffles jumped upon his back, knocking him flat on his face once more. Bunny, buzzing with terror and fury, landed a harsh kick to the man's head that knocked him out. He and Raffles regained their feet, panting, looking each other over. Bunny was astonished by Raffles' fighting prowess, and somewhat surprised at how well he had held his own.

Once their breaths were half-caught, they surveyed the scene, and Raffles said, "We'd better get you fixed up, Bunny boy."

# Chapter Four

B ack in their rented room, Raffles dabbed at Bunny's face with a cool, wet rag. The bleeding had stopped quite quickly, and after examining the gash on his cheek, Raffles had pronounced that Bunny would survive it.

"I confess I'm not much good in a fight," Bunny offered.

"I believe a confession has as its prerequisite a fact which is not already commonly known," Raffles replied, gently joking. Bunny allowed himself a light laugh at his own expense.

Raffles had removed his jacket and waistcoat, laid them on the bed and ran a brush over them, trying to remove the dust and grit left on them from the fight.

"I don't mind telling you, Raffles," Bunny said, beginning to unbutton his shirt cuffs and then his collar, "I'm frightened to stay here at all. I know you've got your plan to get us flush, but—"

Raffles was straight-faced and serious. "You can

face up to it, or run away ashamed. I, for one, can hardly bear the thought of returning to London with nothing in our pockets. You've your gambling debts, and I've to pay for my rooms, club dues, and now it seems I'll need a new jacket. Think about the alternative, Bunny, and tell me then if you don't think we should stay and see this thing through."

Bunny considered. He kept his mouth shut while Raffles hung his jacket and plucked at a waistcoat button which was coming loose. Overcome with a weight of exhaustion, a need to escape the constant barrage in his head of self-recriminations about having let himself spend and gamble his entire inheritance in so short a time, Bunny lay back against the pillows. By then Raffles had removed his shirt and shook the dust from it, folded it and laid it aside.

"I thought, when you said you would help me, and we got on the train," Bunny began, thinking it through even as he spoke the words, "Perhaps I would be able to sort it all out, without the pressure of the city, society..."

"There's nothing to sort, Bunny," Raffles said, and he crumpled the damaged waistcoat in his disgust, and tossed it to a corner of the floor. "You need money, as well as the time required to get it without men who've beaten you—soundly—at cards breathing down the back of your neck. We're safe here, at least, and we can make it on your hundred pounds for a good while, until we can get our hands on enough to square us both up."

They were stood chest-to-chest, near enough that Bunny could smell the echo of their alley-fight coming off the surface of Raffles' skin.

"I suppose you're right," Bunny allowed, "But see where it's gotten us so far."

Raffles touched two fingertips to the small bandage on Bunny's injured cheek, and Bunny flinched.

"Still hurts?" Raffles asked.

"Yes, of course."

"You'll be all right."

"Yes." Bunny caught Raffles by the wrist and kissed the heel of his hand. Raffles smiled, and the tight pit in Bunny's gut melted away.

In a hazy, soft flurry, they finished undressing themselves and each other, and they kissed and kissed—Bunny thought he would never get enough kisses, never be satisfied without just one more—and once Raffles had verified their door was locked, and pulled the curtain on the one small window, they got into bed.

In bed together with AJ Raffles, the famous cricketer and popular party-guest, the object of Bunny's adolescent longings that had persisted well past adolescence—was nowhere Bunny had imagined himself even a handful of nights before. He felt shy as they snuggled beneath the bedclothes, face to face once more, with nothing between them but the warmth they generated. He wished he were bold. He even drew in a hearty breath to steel himself for whatever he might next say or do, but his cowardice and caution overruled his desire.

"Raffles, you—"

"AJ," Raffles corrected him, and stroked the hair over his ear so that Bunny felt the tips of Raffles' fingers against his scalp.

"AJ," Bunny breathed, a murmured intimacy that made him feel all the smaller and more unsure. "You'll have to. . ." he did not even know the words to use. His imagination rolled over his sense, stoked his senses. "Would you mind—?"

Raffles smiled at him then, his rake's smile full of mischief but not at all unkind. "Oh, you dear rabbit," he said, "Have you never?"

"Not— Well. Not much more than what we've already done together."

"Not much more, hm?" Raffles prompted. Then, "*How* much more?"

Bunny tilted his chin to avoid Raffles' eyes, and Raffles fetched him back with a gentle press of fingers against Bunny's face. "Perhaps just show me," he suggested. "No need to speak about it just now."

Raffles moved closer, and his knee brushed Bunny's shin, and he drew Bunny's mouth to his and kissed it sweetly, kissed it open, took his time awakening heat between them. As their kisses deepened, their hands began to roam, and Bunny lost himself in the sensation of being touched, of touching the skin of one whom he had wished to touch for so long. Yielding to Raffles' request for Bunny to show him not that he'd never, but nearly never, he stroked Raffles' naked chest, feeling for muscle-edges, and at last brushed his thumb across the little nipple, pleased to feel it wrinkle up hard and tight almost instantly. He kept it up, a rhythmic sweeping motion, until Raffles shivered.

Bunny resumed stroking the flat of his hand across Raffles' chest, leaning away to get a clear view of his face.

"I like your chin, Raf— *AJ*," he said.

Raffles smiled slightly. "And I like the funny little curl of your ear," he replied, pinching Bunny's ear lobe gently, then folded his hand around Bunny's caressing one. "Is this how much more?" he asked. "It's fine, if it is. We all start somewhere."

Bunny's bashfulness had receded significantly, he felt warm all over, and hectic beneath the skin. He wanted more of Raffles, enough to be bold. When he lowered his hand and found the hard heat of Raffles' prick, the gasp it drew from Raffles took Bunny's own breath away.

"Yes, Bunny," he breathed, and held Bunny's face, and kissed him so intimately Bunny felt the whole of himself somehow. . .*opening*. Raffles whispered between Bunny's parted lips, "Oh yes. . .*yes*. . ."

Raffles reached for Bunny's hand and lifted it, licked it all over until his fingers and palm were wet, then guided it quickly down again. His body rocked up to meet the motion of Bunny's hand, and Bunny felt a surge of thrilling power—that he was able to elicit such a brazen, unguarded response from Raffles was nothing short of beguiling to him —so that he demanded kisses, and took them. He watched Raffles' expression shift from silent bliss to heaving helplessness over the course of moments. Bunny was pleased with himself, in a manner entirely new to him. He felt drunk on it.

"Wait," Raffles blurted urgently, and took hard hold of Bunny's wrist. "Wait, wait." He grinned, breathless. "I don't want to rush."

"Well, I do!" Bunny replied earnestly; he felt desperate to reach that consummatory moment, for Raffles to return his gift in kind. He wanted to stoke in his longed-for friend such a devilish pleasure, and damn the whole world who would condemn them, make criminals of them. Raffles had told him he must go all the way wrong, and Bunny was dying to do just that.

Raffles held his head and tilted it and kissed Bunny's hair at his crown. "You quick rabbit, of course you do. But let me. . ." Raffles spit into his own palm, licked his fingers, and edged the cover away with the side of his hand, then curled his fingers around Bunny's straining, leaky member. "Oh, *Bunny. . .*"

Bunny whimpered and bit his lips, his eyes falling shut and squeezing, then widening behind his closed lids. It was wondrous! His own ministrations brought him dirty pleasure, of course, but this! He clutched at Raffles' waist, fingertips pressing into the edge of the meatier flesh of his rump. This was pure pleasure, everything right, his dear friend whom he had esteemed and dreamed of for so long.

"You excite me," Raffles muttered, his own breath coming in ragged fits and starts, "You lovely thing."

Bunny was heaving, leaning his hip, his chest and belly rising and falling in hot thrums as he gasped for breath like a man drowning.

"How perfectly gorgeous you are," Raffles whispered beside Bunny's face, they were that close, cheek to chin, eyelashes brushing perspiring skin. Bunny felt the wave gather and break, all at once, and he stifled a harsh, shouting cry in the downy pillow. He spilled into Raffles' elegant hand, and felt for him, to bring him along to the same edge of bliss. It took no time at all, barely a slide of Bunny's curled palm, and Raffles shuddered, groaning in a way that to Bunny was pure deliciousness. He wanted to hear that sound—feel it rattle his own chest—and nothing else but that, forever and ever.

Raffles made short, efficient work of cleaning them up, and they lay together still face to face, with entangled ankles and entwined hands. Bunny could feel his smile taking up too much of his face, and closed his lips over his teeth.

"Smile away, my dear fellow," Raffles reassured, his voice low, just they two in all the world and so close they needn't be loud. "I say we'll make a keen duo, henceforth. Do you agree?"

"Team up with you?" Bunny asked, disbelieving of his luck even after what they had just enjoyed together.

"*Partner* with me," Raffles clarified.

"Ah, AJ," Bunny murmured. "I could like nothing better."

Sherlock Holmes sat in Button's tavern, having long since finished his brandy and smoked four cigarettes, at a small table with a view of the door. A check of his pocket watch confirmed his humiliation; AJ Raffles had failed to appear at the appointed hour, and failed again at the stroke of the following one. Before the next hour could circle round, Holmes gathered his coat, avoided all eyes, and left.

"Perhaps, after all, we could just stay here, in Sheepmeadow," Bunny mused. They lay fitted together like folded fabric, curled around each other and tucked in tight. "It's not so bad a place."

"You must have a better relationship than I do

with the supposedly idyllic country village, Bunny, to suggest such a thing." Raffles' lips brushed the back edge of Bunny's ear as he spoke, and while he was in the neighbourhood, he pressed a kiss there, as well.

"Well, there's no one here I'm in debt to," Bunny replied. "And there's no such thing as the Albany, I realise, but we could find a nice apartment for you."

Raffles laughed softly through his nose. "It's a lovely dream, Bunny, but that's all it is, a dream. Small places like this are full of gossip and backstabbing, there's no such thing as a private life. And I should say I require one."

"A private life?"

"Yes, of course. It's easy enough for a gentleman of a certain bent to conduct his personal affairs in the city—even in society—without much suspicion, merely by being charming and keeping a clean reputation," Raffles said, lecturing but without condescension. "In a village like this? There's too much daylight, my dear boy. When what is needed is shadows, and plenty of them."

Bunny thought this over, and hummed as he thought. "I suppose you may be right."

"I know I am." Raffles brushed his palm over Bunny's body, from low belly to chest, right up to his throat, and down again, and Bunny felt adoration in the touch. "Anyway, in no time we'll have our money and your worries will be behind you. Then it's nothing but costume balls and cards rooms and the Turkish baths."

"And cricket!" Bunny added, with a grin.

"Yes, and cricket. That reputation I mentioned. The more visible one's superficialities, the less likely others are to look deeper. And that will serve us well."

"I trust you," Bunny murmured, and his eyes were heavy though he wanted to fight sleep so he could lay awake in Raffles' embrace until morning forced them to part.

"I'm glad of it. You won't regret it. Sleep, now, you rabbit, or I'll have you again."

Bunny shivered at the thought. "Oh, Raffles!" he gusted, forgetting he was to call him AJ now that they were more intimately acquainted.

Raffles laughed and kissed the back of his neck, and moved his hand again, but this time instead of sweeping upward, he reached down. Bunny could fend off sleep just a bit longer—easily.

# Chapter Five

**N**ext morning, Sherlock Holmes found himself resentful of every discomfort and inconvenience. Having to dress in proper clothes to leave inferior rented rooms to eat an inferior breakfast in a truly inferior tavern affronted him. The thin, tepid coffee appalled him. He was indignant at the weather, fuming over the broken yolks of his eggs. He shoved the plate away with both hands, huffing his disgust.

"You seem terribly out of sorts, Holmes." Watson stated the obvious through half a mouthful of toast. "Did you not sleep well?"

"I would have slept beautifully had I not been made to wait up for—" Holmes caught himself. "A message that never came."

"Was it not that socialite, Raffles, you were waiting for last night?"

Holmes frowned, having held some hope that perhaps if Watson had not truly forgotten his appointment to walk out with Raffles, at least he would have the compassion to pretend he'd forgotten. Alas, it seemed Holmes would not be allowed the comfort of a lie designed to erase the recent past.

"True enough. But it was not meant to be," Holmes replied, funneling the disappointment of his abandonment by the charming and handsome AJ Raffles into a stage-worthy sigh. "Instead I drank cheap whisky and smoked too many cigarettes, and saw nothing at all of the village."

Watson gestured with his cutlery. "I told you his reputation is poor. Now add rudeness to his list of character defects."

"He seemed interesting, Watson. That's all." Holmes had nearly convinced himself, and shed his dark cloud in favour of new resolve to move forward. A morning paper was what he needed, to delve into and find something no one else but he would recognise as fascinating. To his detriment, however—as Holmes raised his head to crane around looking for a Times or even a Courier-Call, if that was all there was to be had—in sidled none other than the degenerate, rakish Mr Raffles, and the young companion who looked at Raffles as if he had singlehandedly hung the stars, as well as the moon. Holmes's mood instantly soured and he sank back in his chair with narrowed eyes and clenched jaw.

As the two passed the small table where Watson's plate sat empty while Holmes' had merely been picked at, they stopped and offered polite greetings and handshakes. Raffles' friend launched into an over-detailed retelling of an encounter with hoodlums, to which Watson paid rapt attention; Watson liked fights. Holmes touched Raffles' cuff to catch his full attention, and said in a low voice, "I waited for you last night, Mr Raffles."

"I was so terribly afraid you would," Raffles said, with alluring regret in his tone. "I apologise profusely, my dear Mr Holmes. Something came up." He gestured toward his friend, on whose face was a small bandage below his left eye. What such a thing could possibly have to do with him, or with Raffles missing their appointed meeting time, Holmes could not discern.

A burst of brightness flashed through the front door just then, in the person of Miss Irene Adler, whose face portrayed consternation and whose eyes sparked with ferocity. There seemed—to Sherlock Holmes, at least—to be an air of thrilling unpredictability, bordering on outright chaos, to everything Miss Adler did or said. Despite this tendency toward small-scale mayhem, her mind was keener than those of most men Holmes had met (and far more so than any woman's). He wondered if the former was cultivated as a way of disarming targets of the latter. She was useful, and amusing. Watson was green-eyed with jealousy around her and professed not to see any of the appeal Holmes did.

"Dr Watson, Sherlock," she fluttered, smacking

her handbag down on their table and yanking at the fingers of her gloves. "I waited for a certain gentleman last night for two hours. Two hours! Normally to hear of any woman wasting so much time for a man who has made her no promises would send me raving, and here I find myself engaging in just that same bit of foolishness. All on your behalf, Sherlock," she scolded, barely stopping for breath as the gentlemen around her shrank and looked away, unsure how to behave in the presence of a woman—*the* woman—who would dare to storm unannounced and uninvited into their circle and speak so plainly. "I don't know how I can possibly get hands on that man's diary if he won't even be bothered to keep to it! I saw him write me down in it. Well, not me, but the name I gave."

"I have every faith in you, Miss Adler," Holmes said coolly. Watson tried to hide a rolling of his eyes toward heaven but Holmes caught it.

"Are you not going to eat that, Sherlock?" Miss Adler inquired, pointing with her now-naked finger at his plate. Holmes gestured she could have it, and as Raffles looked around for a chair for her, Irene Adler lifted away Holmes' breakfast plate and retreated to another table.

Just when his fellows were about to sigh their relief that she had left them, she called out. "Oh, Mr Manders! Do you remember—we met and chatted? You dear man. Would you do me the favour of retrieving my little velvet bag that I've left there by

Dr Watson's elbow? I'll need my coin to pay for my tea. And—hello, madam, aren't you the landlady? Might I have a pot of tea, and a pitcher of that beautiful milk that has made this village so famous?"

She was brilliant; of course the village was as plain as parchment, and its cows had no particular renown, but the woman smiled with pride to think a society lady from London admired the town, as well as its resident cows. Miss Adler's fingers, bare or gloved, always had several souls wrapped around them.

As Raffles' friend left Holmes' and Watson's table for Miss Adler's, she was heard to coo, "Oh, dear me, Mr Manders—what's happened to your handsome face?" and Holmes wondered how she would manage her fork and knife with yet another gentleman curled up in her tidy little palm.

"He cut himself shaving," said Raffles drily, to no one in particular. Holmes laughed lightly under his breath. "Join me for a smoke by the fire, Holmes?"

Not forgetting his humiliation of the previous evening, but certainly putting less stock in it, Holmes agreed and the two moved to the pair of armchairs by the fire. It did not escape Holmes' notice that Raffles inched his chair closer to Holmes' as he lowered himself into it.

"I'd like to make it up to you," Raffles said, as he leaned to offer Holmes his matchbox. "Will you consider allowing me the opportunity?"

Holmes felt a flush across his chest, and he hid his face with the hand lighting his cigarette, for fear of appearing overeager to forgive. Raffles was silky and disarming; Holmes wished he could think his manners and smiles were a disguise, but he seemed genuine—regardless of what Watson had said about his partiality to bad company. Holmes himself was considered by many to be the very worst company one could be in, and he did not have the benefit of being so handsome or agreeable as AJ Raffles, so it seemed unkind for Holmes to refuse him.

"What do you have in mind?"

"I understand there's a quite scenic lake nearby, perhaps we might take in the views."

Holmes nodded before he had even decided to agree. After a moment his voice followed along and he said, "Clean country air never did any harm."

"Fantastic," Raffles replied, and he really did look pleased. He flicked the spent tip of his cigarette into an ashtray on the table between them and cast a glance back at the table they'd left, where Watson was sitting with his arms folded across his chest, looking hard in their direction. "Your friend certainly keeps a close watch on you," Raffles commented.

Holmes nodded, smiling. "Yes, that's my Watson," he said, as ever feeling no need to disguise his fondness.

Raffles hummed, perhaps disapprovingly but in

an instant he was on his feet, smiling away at Holmes, reaching to shake his hand. Holmes obliged, meeting his gaze, and what Holmes saw in Raffles' eyes was unmistakable and shocking, and gave Holmes another hot flush. "I shall look forward to seeing you again, Mr Holmes."

"I feel the same, Mr Raffles."

With a playful smirk on his lips, Raffles turned away. "Come on, Bunny," he commanded, and his friend rose quickly to follow him out of the tavern without question, and with barely a goodbye to Miss Adler, whose table he had been stood by, as if keeping sentry over her while she ate Holmes' breakfast and drank her milky tea.

Raffles and Holmes had nearly circled the lake; there was a well-worn path through fields turned beige with autumn's early tinges of cold, and thickets of trees still crowned with their red and gold leaves. Around a bend, they came upon a clearing with a placid view of the water and a little tree-capped island. Two wooden benches invited lingering. Raffles had guided their conversation; knowing how every man's favourite topic was himself, he had asked Holmes about his work as a detective, his recent interesting cases.

"I'd have been back in London days ago, but for the fact of my brother assigning me a particularly secret matter, of some documents which seem to have fallen into wrong hands on their journey from Africa. I understand they're accompanied by some jewels, but those are of no interest."

Raffles felt a bit giddy that Holmes had brought up the rumoured cache of rubies and diamonds he'd caught wind of, without Raffles even prompting him.

"I doubt there's many who prefer papers to gemstones, Holmes," Raffles gently chided, then turned serious and caught Holmes' pale-eyed gaze. "But then, you're not one of the many. Rather, you're absolutely one of a kind."

He thought Holmes might have blushed, and if he had, it did no harm to his unique, slender features.

Turning back to the topic at hand, Raffles asked, "What about thieves?" He struck a match to light their cigarettes. Holmes steadied Raffles' hand with his fingers against its back, and his thumb unmistakably stroked the center of Raffles' palm.

"What about them?" Holmes replied.

"Well, I assume there must be some common fatal error, the discovery of which helps you to catch your man?" Raffles had peppered their chat with such pointed phrases, hoping to plant seeds in Holmes' brilliant head which might later bloom into something Raffles might reap.

"Not at all," Holmes said thoughtfully. "In fact,

quite the inverse is true. Every thief worth a far-thing has his own individual signature. Discernment of this little telltale flourish can lead me right to him."

Raffles half-smiled. "Well, isn't that fascinating," he said. "I'd never have thought of it."

Holmes hummed. After a moment, he said, "I must confess, Raffles, I'm a little disappointed in *your* skill at discernment, or lack thereof."

Raffles widened his eyes in response to the little insult, but grinned. "Whatever can I have missed?" he asked, defending. "I complimented your suit, and I'm carrying your brand of cigarettes."

"You seem to have missed out on my buttonhole," Holmes told him. "Do you know how near-impossible it was to find a green carnation in this tiny edge of nowhere?"

Of course, Raffles had immediately noticed the little dyed-green blossom pinned to Holmes' lapel, but had purposely said nothing about it. It served him to let Holmes simmer a while, so that Raffles could garner his trust as well as tease out information.

Removing his overcoat and draping it over the wooden bench for a blanket, he invited Holmes to sit, then joined him, his arm propped on the bench's back behind Holmes' shoulder, and pressed his thigh alongside Holmes'. "Forgive me another blunder," Raffles said quietly. He had tossed away his cigarette, and now plucked the short end of Holmes' from between his fingers, and flicked it away toward the edge of the lake. As he turned toward Holmes once more, he let his hand come to rest on Holmes' knee.

He'd meant to initiate a kiss, but it seemed Holmes had the same impulse, because it was not at all clear who kissed whom. Holmes wrapped his long, fine hand around Raffles' there on his knee, and Raffles drew back just enough to wet his lips with the point of his tongue. Another kiss, this one quicker but more urgent—Holmes was self-assured and somehow coarser than Raffles had expected— and only when they were nearing breathlessness did Raffles pull away. He dragged the tip of one finger over the corners of his mouth.

"So, your friend Doctor Watson," Raffles ventured. "Or?"

"No," Holmes replied, with something in it like regret. "Nothing like it. I've known men of our kind, of course. But not known them intimately." Raffles got his meaning. There were always encounters to be had, in the baths, or in the shadows—Raffles knew the places as well as he knew the houses where all the best parties were held during the height of the season—but to have a lover in the body-and-soul sense was a rarer prize, and not one every man of their kind, as Holmes had put it, was willing to chance.

"I see," Raffles said, and Holmes still held his hand, but all at once released it, as if remembering himself. "I can't say whether I'm sad for you, or relieved on my own behalf."

"I venture it's possible to be both," Holmes said with a small, thin smile that Raffles took as encouragement.

Leaning over just enough, Raffles caught up a small stone from beside his boot, and let it fly. It landed in the still lake with a satisfying, round *plop*, and sent out its orbiting ripples.

"I enjoy those rings," Holmes mused. "An eloquent expression without words. That everything one does, or says, or perhaps even thinks, has multitudinous effects."

Raffles leaned in close and pressed his lips to the side of the long, tight-collared neck, with tingly longing to unfasten the collar and kiss from jaw to clavicle, and back again. His lips found a spot Holmes had missed while shaving—just a few bristly whiskers—and he scraped his lower lip sideways, feeling the skin catch. In a moment, Holmes had shifted, and their arms wound around, and their kisses were greedier than before. Holmes' breath became louder, and he slid a hand beneath Raffles' jacket, scratching at the buttons of his waistcoat as if to tear them free of their threads.

Abruptly, Raffles broke away, and even stood, pacing a short path in front of the bench, while

Holmes studied him with narrow eyes. Raffles had meant to get information, to make a friend of a man who was a friend of the police. Sherlock Holmes was useful to him. But now there was something interfering with Raffles' calculations.

"Have you any idea why I invited you out here?" Raffles murmured, wanting to bite his tongue against the urge to confess his motives. Holmes only looked at him expectantly, waiting for Raffles to explain himself. A shake of his head, and Raffles muttered, "Now I'm beginning to wonder, myself." He smoothed his clothes and offered Holmes a hand. "We should finish our walk. I can think of a few people bound to miss us."

# Chapter Six

Back in time for tea, Raffles and Holmes parted ways outside the tavern. Holmes walked on toward his hotel, while Raffles went inside to inquire of the landlady where in the village he might have the fallen button sewn back on his waistcoat. He found Dr Watson stood by the bar, with a nearly-empty tumbler of whisky in front of him. He lifted his chin when he caught sight of Raffles, and mused, "Well, well. If it isn't little Bunny's keeper!" He sounded jocular but Raffles did not know him well enough to decide if he was being joked with, or about. Before he could reply beyond a quick nod, Watson went on. "I rather think he won't need you to keep him anymore; Miss Irene Adler was here earlier."

Watson raised an eyebrow and drained his glass.

"Miss Adler, you say," Raffles said, keeping his voice cool while alarm bells clanged in his head. "Might you know where Miss Adler is in residence?"

Watson let go a round, sarcastic laugh. "There's

a woman called Sister Frances with a house at the end of this block. Number 60. Perhaps you've noticed its red door, during your strolls about town." He snorted again. "Miss Adler has taken a room there. And a number of other ladies as well."

Raffles twisted his lip; Watson put him off —calling him Bunny's mother when he himself seemed both guard- and lapdog to Sherlock Holmes. "You've met one, yourself?" he asked pointedly.

"Not this time around," Watson smirked back. "Country girls always send one away with unasked-for souvenirs. That, or they want a train ticket to London and a new monogram for their handkerchiefs. I'm not looking for a plague—of either sort."

Raffles nodded once more, then made haste to the end of the block. The red door of number 60 was easily opened and slipped into; as Raffles had expected, the foyer and parlour were done up in more garish crimson shades, with a patterned carpet and heavy velvet drapes on the windows. From a closed door further down the entry hall emerged a man and woman with their heads ducked close; they kissed and the man set his hat low on his forehead, scuttling past Raffles with a clear disinclination toward being acknowledged. The woman, in a silk dressing gown and with her hair undone despite it being nearly half-past two in the afternoon, fluttered her fingers at him, and smiled coyly before vanishing behind her closing door.

Raffles steeled himself with a steadying breath, and charged to the one remaining closed door in his view. He opened it quietly, unsure whether he was leery of or enticed by what vision might await him on the other side, of his dear Bunny and the handsome, brassy Miss Adler in any number of scandalous arrangements. The one he found them in, however, surprised him.

"Miss Adler, I think you overestimate your worth."

She turned with shock evident on her face. Sitting with one bent leg up on the bed, the other dangling, with all her blouse buttons undone down to the top edge of her undergarment, Miss Adler held Bunny's billfold in one hand and a ten-pound note in the other. Bunny lay beside her, all dressed, snoring. On the bedside table stood a bottle and two glasses, one still mostly full.

"Half that amount should be more than enough," Raffles told her, frowning deeply, clenching his hands behind his back. "to cover the cost of the liquour." He tipped his head toward Bunny's slack body.

Miss Adler looked as if considering whether to argue or negotiate, then assessed her chance to get past him and flee the room. In the end, she replaced the note in the wallet and withdrew another of a smaller denomination. Scowling fiercely, she threw the billfold at Raffles, who caught it against his chest, then counted the notes inside. With a scowl of his own, he stepped forward and thrust his hand inside the edge of her blouse, withdrawing a missing ten-pound note, warm from having been nestled against her breast.

In a flash, she grabbed the bottle off the nightstand and swung her arm back, menacing him. Raffles did not flinch, and—recognising her bluff was called—Miss Adler lowered her arm, and let the empty bottle land on the bed. She tucked her fiver deep inside her blouse.

Bunny still lay insensate across the bed, and Raffles began to rearrange him, at last getting an arm under each of Bunny's shoulders, and dragging him backward until he got him drowsily to his feet. Tossing one of Bunny's arms over his shoulder and catching his wrist to balance him, Raffles wound an arm around his waist and leaned into his hip. "Oh, Bunny," he moaned, "You're going to be the death of me."

Back in their shabby rented room, Raffles heaped Bunny onto the bed semi-upright against the pillows, then dragged up his legs and began loosening his shoelaces. As he worked the shoes off one by one and set them on the floor, Bunny began at last to come around.

"You rabbit," Raffles scolded, "I drag and half-carry you up one street, around the corner, and two-thirds of the way up another, and you can't be bothered to wake up. But now you're propped up like the prince of Persia while I remove your boots like a servant—"

"Thank you, AJ."

Caught up short by the smallness of Bunny's voice, and the sincere expression of gratitude, Raffles was like a toy balloon leaking air. He sat on the edge of the bed next to Bunny's hip with a softening spine.

"I'd do it again," Raffles told him, "But don't make me."

"I won't. I'll try not to." Bunny reached for his hand, but Raffles withdrew it and fished Bunny's wallet out of the inside pocket of his jacket, and tossed it in a slow arc so that Bunny was able to catch it with a clap of his hands.

"How are you feeling, then?"

"Bit crooked, still," Bunny confessed. He set aside the billfold and reached for Raffles' hand once more. "Lie down with me."

Raffles grinned, and drew Bunny's hand up to his mouth to kiss his fingers.

"I think I'm annoyed with you," Raffles said lamely. "You've put me through a great deal of trouble."

Instead of looking cowed, Bunny grinned devil-ishly, and Raffles was delighted. "How can I make it up to you?" Bunny asked. His eyes were glassy.

"Don't tempt me to take advantage of a man under the influence," Raffles said, though in hon-esty with himself, he saw little chance of being dis-suaded from accepting any invitation to sin his dear rabbit might offer.

"Please do," Bunny murmured, and his pouting lower lip was more than Raffles could bear. He must quickly find a way to make it right, and as Bunny began shedding clothing with steady hands, inspir-ation struck.

"Let me please you," Raffles said urgently. "Let me adore you."

"Dear god," Bunny breathed, and scrambled up to sit, put his hands on Raffles' neck and arm, and kissed him with a wine-sweet mouth. "My head's spinning. Not from the drink."

"I believe you," Raffles whispered.

Moments later, they were both undressed and Bunny lay beneath him. His sweet belly, the pale down of hair on his thighs and chest, his delicate hands Raffles wanted to dress in wristwatches and rings—and would, he vowed it to himself then and there—all given over so freely to Raffles' ministra-tions he felt the weight of the world upon him. He must repay the honour with pleasure, and damned if he would fail his dear boy, this rabbit, for whom he felt things he'd felt for no other. His heart thwacked in its cage of ribs; the breath in his mouth felt full of fire as it passed his lips.

Raffles kissed and kissed, lingering at the base of Bunny's throat, inside his elbow, the abdomen that sunk away from his lips and tongue on a lovely, startled gasp.

"Is there nothing about you that isn't soft and sweet?" Raffles marveled, and Bunny's response was an exquisite sigh.

By the time Raffles' roaming mouth neared his flank and the crease between belly and thigh, Bunny was thrumming taut, and Raffles swept hands beneath his hips to smooth along the plump backside; Bunny raised his hips to give him space. Raffles rubbed his nose against Bunny's thigh, and then his lips, and at last opened his mouth to kiss and taste, the tip of his tongue drawing a swirling path that made Bunny mew and cry and bite the heel of his hand. His desire was beautifully obvious in the roll of his pelvis, let alone the rampant state of his pale-pink prick. Raffles nosed his way up the sweet tummy to his navel and teased it with nose and lips, and Bunny gave an affectionate laugh and touched Raffles' face.

Raffles looked up, and Bunny looked down, and they shared a getting-away-with-it grin, and Raffles knew he had found his perfect ally and companion. "We shall be lifelong friends, I think," he mused aloud.

"I hope so," Bunny smiled at him.

"Are you happy?"

"Oh, my dear AJ. . .you've not the slightest idea how happy I am."

Raffles felt a warm flush all through him, and lay a sweet, gentle kiss below Bunny's tummy button, just above the riotous patch of crinkly pale hair, and was overwhelmed by his desire—not to please himself, for a change, but to please Bunny—to make his affection known, to share heat, to bring his friend to the brink of bliss, and tip him over it.

Everything in him was straining with desire, and rather than let it burn him up, Raffles used it as fuel. He would set this man alight.

Shutting his eyes, Raffles let his other senses lead him—the scent of Bunny's desire, the slide of silky skin beneath Raffles' caressing fingers, and, oh!, the taste of him salt-dark on Raffles' tongue and between his hungry lips. He lapped and suckled, kissing and kissing, swallowed, could not suppress a groan, endeavoured to make Bunny as drunk with pleasure as he had earlier been on cheap booze. He kept his lips wet, his tongue soft, his throat open to drink him down—this pretty man whom he wanted to please as he had never before wanted to please anyone but himself. His wish to worship Bunny was hot and selfish.

Bunny let go wild, whimpering noises, spurring Raffles on and on even as his jaw and throat ached. He wanted to feel used-up, as proof of his success. Bunny's hands touching his face and tangling in the errant waves of his hair were earned currency, hard-won evidence of the rightness of his cause. He gratefully drank down bitterness for the sake of his companion's rapturous response.

"Oh, I want to kiss you," Bunny sighed. "AJ, I must kiss you!"

So commanded, Raffles raised himself to his knees between Bunny's dropped-open thighs, caged Bunny between his hands, licked his own mouth clean, and settled in to offer his kisses in sweet veneration. Bunny's tongue thrust into Raffles' mouth, all force and urgency, and Raffles met him there, open-lipped and passionate. Echoing the harsh demand in their kisses, they thrust together and against each other, found a pleasing rhythm and grind. Bunny kissed him breathless, then Raffles gasped against his upturned jaw.

What had begun in elevated reverence quickly, thrillingly, devolved into a hot clutch, chest to chest, Raffles grunting and Bunny mewling. The music of their held and heaving breath, their voices half-stifled against closed lips and each other's bitten shoulders, had Raffles at the brink all too quickly, and he looked to Bunny's exquisite angel-face to be sure he would not arrive too far ahead. Bunny's eyes were shut, his mouth was open, his neck arched beautifully.

"My love," Raffles gasped, rough lips dry against that pale, vulnerable throat, and in the span of a few more rough breaths, Bunny thrummed beneath him, his thighs gripping tight against Raffles' hips, and the hot spill between them let Raffles know he had done well to please him. He let go a hot breath in the hollow of Bunny's shoulder, and slip-slid hard and hot, racing to rise up and meet him, so they could fall together, back to earth. Finding his peak was easy; Bunny's fingers clutched at his flanks and he groaned in sympathy as Raffles bit back cries.

In the warm woolen moments after, Raffles kissed Bunny's fingertips one by one, and Bunny gazed tenderly at him, eyes still slow-blinking with inebriation.

"Bunny, I want to tell you all there is to know."

"What, *all?*" Bunny's eyes widened, and he grinned.

"All there is to know about me," Raffles clarified, and brushed the pad of Bunny's thumb across his bottom lip, back and forth, soft.

"I want to go wrong with you, Raffles," Bunny said. "I mean, AJ. Will I ever get used to saying it?"

"Keep saying it and it will come naturally," Raffles assured him. "There's perhaps more wrong than you realise."

Bunny looked puzzled and expectant.

"I told you I'm hard up," Raffles said. "How do you think I pay for my rooms at the Albany? Savile Row suits and memberships at clubs. Can you even being to imagine where my money comes from?"

"I thought you must have inherited," Bunny shrugged. "Or your people are well-to-do." He appeared to think it over. "I came in for money and spent it all; perhaps you did the same foolish thing as me."

"Far more foolish, I'm afraid," Raffles told him. "But then again."

"Then again?"

"I have rather a lot of fun, Bunny," Raffles confessed, smiling against Bunny's knuckles.

"I like to have fun. And now I'm mad with curiosity; you must tell me at once."

"You may not believe it, Bunny, but I thieve jewels and artworks—and cash, too—to support my upscale style of life."

Bunny let go a little gasp that would have been beautiful in their previous context, but which was then a sign of true shock. "Well, I *don't* believe it! You, a cracksman? Gentlemen don't steal for their living."

"This one does, I'm afraid." Raffles had no regrets and no intention to change his habits. "I felt I should tell you before we fall too far in together; it seems only fair you should know everything."

"You're joking," Bunny asserted. Raffles assured him he was not, and went on to reference several of the recent season's most talked-about thefts: a sapphire tiara worn by the *duchesse du Printemps* at her wedding to old Snooty Woodthorn; a collection of priceless coins from the study of Dr Edward St Edmunds; the Francisco diamonds.

"All done by the same burglar, and that burglar —friend rabbit—was me." Raffles could not repress his self-satisfied smile. As much fun as he'd had safe-breaking, lockpicking, and sneaking up trellises and down rope ladders in the moonlight—not to mention the social maneuvers required to keep himself above suspicion—he found even more novel sport in confiding it all to Bunny.

He could see Bunny's expression changing as he thought it over, took it all in. A flicker of terror threatened to burst hot into a flame at the thought not that Bunny might go to the police or speak ill of Raffles in society, but that he may reject Raffles as too unprincipled or immoral a man with which to keep company. The silence stretched on, and Raffles folded Bunny's dear hands up inside his own, holding on for dear life, his fear growing with each heartbeat.

At last, Bunny asked brightly, "Can I help?"

# Chapter Seven

**W**atson was eating soft-cooked eggs and reading a severely-folded newspaper when Holmes joined him at the tavern. "At last, he rises," Watson said jovially, and pressed a chair away from the table with is foot against its leg, inviting Holmes to join him. "How do you do this morning, Holmes?"

"Very well, in manners physical and psychical," Holmes replied quickly. "However, I feel a certain alignment with the caged panther; no room to run, nothing new to see. Soon I may have little choice but to bite the hand that feeds me."

As he closed his metaphor, Holmes noticed that Watson had arranged a bun and jam on a saucer and placed it before him.

"I beg you not to, Holmes," Watson intoned. "I'm still smarting from the last round."

"You wear that jacket well, Watson. You should wear it more often."

His dear friend looked chuffed and slightly embarrassed, and Holmes basked in it.

"What will it take for us to be freed of your brother Mycroft's heavy thumb?" Watson asked. "For that's what keeps us in this village, unless I am greatly mistaken."

"Not at all, Watson. You are quite correct. Try as I have, I cannot flush out my quarry. The trouble with small towns is that people are suspicious of strangers, even moreso ones from the city. Triple that for anyone who appears educated beyond the basic levels. Even in disguise, I am too easily marked out as an interloper, and thus am met with nothing but tightly closed mouths."

"There is always Miss Adler," Watson suggested, though the pain it brought him to do so was obvious; he considered her an unscrupulous viper.

"She reports little more success than I have had," Holmes replied, and dipped the tip of his knife in the jam, lay it carefully upon a torn-off morsel of the bun. With his mouth full, he added, "She suspects the man who's been watching me is a toady of Moriarty's."

Watson sat up straighter, broadening his solid frame in soldier-still readiness. "For what purpose?" he demanded. The man Holmes had so casually referenced was one they both knew to be at the very pinnacle of crime, a brilliant and dangerous adversary to the great detective.

Holmes thought to reassure and calm his friend,

but found he could not bring himself to soften the man out of such an appealing state of excitement. "Oh, probably to murder me." Holmes smirked and waved it away with a flick of his fingers. Watson practically growled. Still relishing his low-boiling fury, Holmes soothed, "I jest, dear boy. More likely, he has been sent to pilfer the very documents I am after."

Before there could be further discussion of the matter, the front door opened, which set its little bell ringing, and Holmes looked up to see AJ Raffles and his companion, Mr Manders, entering. Holmes caught Raffles' eye and motioned an invitation to share the table with him and Watson. Once greetings were exchanged and the newcomers had claimed chairs and signaled the landlady to bring them breakfast, Holmes turned to Raffles.

"Being a sportsman, as you are, Raffles," he began, "I wonder—can I infer that you are the adventurous type?"

"It's not a word I've ever applied to myself, nor heard another apply to me, but. . ." His face lit up with amused pleasure. "Why, yes, I'd say it suits me well." Raffles wore one of the seductive smiles Holmes had come to appreciate—whether he wished to or not.

"I wonder if I might persuade you—and you, too, Mr Manders—to join Watson and me in some clandestine work on my current case. Where two sets of eyes and two sets of hands have failed, I suspect doubling our number just might prove the very thing for it." He fixed his gaze upon Raffles' handsome face as he spoke, only sparing a quick glance toward his friend.

"I can't imagine we could possibly be of use to you, Mr Holmes. Me, a sometime cricketer and rest-of-the-time layabout—" Holmes felt Raffles' easy self-deprecation was a subtle way of reminding others of his specialness, as if inviting them to correct him, and yet could not help but be charmed by the ploy, even as he saw straight through it. "And Bunny having no particular occupation at all. I'm sure you need a professional's touch. Perhaps the local police."

Holmes let out a laugh. "I have met the local constables, Mr Raffles, and while they seem competent to the level necessary to keep the local goats out of the way of the carriages, I think what I require is probably beyond their ability."

"Even still, I think we must decline. Ah, what is better to begin a new day but a perfectly beautiful egg and a hot cup of coffee, eh, Bunny?" Raffles looked truly admiring of the breakfast plate set before him by the landlady. "I thank you, madam." Her cheeks reddened as she left them.

Holmes regrouped and tried another angle. "Watson, perhaps you can persuade the gentlemen of our need for the assistance."

"If Holmes says he needs you, rest assured, gentlemen, he is not prone to empty flattery, and so certainly does have need of your particular—what? —talents. Skills. Knowledge."

"Bunny and I don't intend to stay very long in Sheepmeadow, I'm afraid," Raffles replied. Holmes could see this assertion was brand new information for young Mr Manders, whose face was as easy to read as his own dear friend Watson's was.

Holmes felt a pang of disappointment, and found an excuse to send Watson away—a pointless errand to discover whether the local bank was visible from the rail track as it passed behind their hotel (Holmes already knew it was not, and either way it mattered not a wit). Manders, eager and with imagination enough to think everything in which Holmes was involved was bound to be on the thin edge of wild excitement, invited himself along with Watson, which served Holmes' purpose perfectly.

"I am terribly disappointed to hear that you will be leaving soon," Holmes offered. "Would that I could persuade you to stay, but assisting on my case was, I'm afraid, the very best offer I could make, and unfortunately was not enough to tempt you."

"Oh, I don't know," Raffles said lightly, with that devil-in-it half-smirk Holmes found all but irresistible. "I imagine you have at least one better offer." He gave Holmes a pointed look, and the reaction it elicited in him was particularly stirring. Holmes crossed one thigh over the other and felt his coat all over, searching for cigarettes.

Before Holmes could offer a retort, a shadow fell across the table and the scarred man he'd seen repeatedly in the previous days was stood there, looming by virtue not so much of his height—which was not exceptional—but of his closeness.

"You Sherlock Holmes?" the man gruffed out.

Holmes steadied himself outwardly, though in truth he was unnerved. "The very one," he affirmed. "How may I help you?"

"Got some information I think will interest you."

"All information interests me," Holmes replied, "At least at first. May I inquire—"

All at once, Raffles—in a tone and accent as uncouth and seaworthy as the scarred man's—put in, "Mr 'olmes is a very busy man. Wotever you got a say to 'im, you c'n just as well say to me."

A glance in Raffles' direction left Holmes dumbfounded; his posture had changed to match the voice, and somehow even his clothing looked shabbier. Holmes prided himself on his gift for remaking himself with costumes, false hair, and put-on accents, but he was as nothing compared to the illusion Raffles had conjured in a few seconds, without any of the usual accoutrements.

"I'm talkin' to Mr Holmes. Who'dya think *you*

are?"

Raffles threw down his fork—but kept hold of his knife—and leapt to his feet, sending the man a half-step backward. "I'm the one wot's tellin' you that if you want to talk wiv Mr 'olmes, you send a note and request an appointment for some of the gen'leman's time, like a decent fella. And not come round 'ere interruptin' a man's breakfast and talkin' outcher neck about some mysterious this-or-that." As Raffles spoke, the scarred man moved back and back, by measures, until Raffles was stood between him and Holmes. "Now, if you please." He tilted his head. "Leave the gen'leman in peace to finish his meal."

The man, scowling, drew a short breath as if he might respond in kind to Raffles' hard talk, but the landlady was by then hovering nearby, and was as no-nonsense a person as one would expect to run a village tavern, which in its later hours was likely a second home to the aimless and those given to over-indulgence in drink. In short, she looked quite capable of dispensing with any ruckus that may arise from two men barking through gritted teeth at half-past ten in the morning.

The man with the scar said nothing, but gave Raffles a penetrating gaze full of fury before turning on his heel and leaving. Raffles cleared his throat and sniffed, reassembled his own elegant posture, and resumed his seat. He fired a triumphant expression at Holmes.

"By jove, that was what I call a very fine display," Holmes said with enthusiasm and no small amount of envy.

"I fancied myself a thespian, back in my school days," Raffles said dismissively, but Holmes could see he was pleased to have received the praise. Tilting his head toward the door, he offered, "Perhaps you'd like company on your walk back to your hotel? I know from recent experience that beasts of that sort will tend to linger in dark doorways and down alleys."

Holmes' automatic response was to decline; he had methods at his disposal which could disarm a thug, evade a garotte, or put a man flat out on the pavement, and was never fearful to engage them when necessary. Intrigued as he was—and had been since the first—by AJ Raffles, though, Holmes instead agreed that he would, indeed, very much appreciate Raffles escorting him back to his rooms.

As the two emerged from the tavern, they met the returning Watson and Manders, the former looking serious as ever, and the latter smiling overmuch and even a bit breathless.

"Mr Holmes, we looked from every angle—I even had Dr Watson give me a leg up so I'd be more like the right height—looking out from the train window," he reported.

"Very clever," Holmes praised. "And what did you discover?"

"Not a thing!"

Watson shook his head. "There's no way to see the bank from the train. We walked half a mile and could not once get it in our sights."

Holmes clapped Watson on the back, then offered Manders a handshake. "Well done, my friends. To have it confirmed by two such trusted gentlemen means I can move on with my theory."

Both Watson and Manders reacted to the praise and gratitude, with puffed-up grins and silent self-congratulation.

"Bunny, I'll have to meet you later; Mr Holmes and I are going to walk a bit," Raffles reported. The four men by then had moved away from the tavern door so as not to block it. An unmistakable, red-lipped bustling drew their attention back to the entrance as Irene Adler stormed up to the door; she waved her gloved hand in their direction.

Raffles' white teeth showed in a mirthful smile. "Never fear, my friend," he said to Bunny, "Clearly you won't be by yourself for long."

It had taken more than one reassurance from Holmes for Dr Watson to surrender him to Raffles. It was clear Watson did not trust him, eyed him with suspicion even as Raffles employed nearly his entire arsenal of friendliness and charm. Raffles could not blame him—after all, he was not wrong to be mistrustful, given that Raffles was, in fact, running a confidence game on his friend Sherlock Holmes —but he also could not but take slight offense. Holmes was in no danger from him, and while Raffles found he did not need to rely entirely on ruse when it came to drawing Holmes into a sort of holiday romance, now that he had Bunny—for whom he held a long-burning candle—Raffles imagined a brokenhearted Holmes might serve Watson well. The candle Watson held for Holmes was not entirely well-hidden.

Once they were free, though, Raffles had offered to walk Holmes the long way round, and so they slow-strolled by the scenic lake, arm in arm.

"I understand you are in society," Holmes said. "I, myself, live a rather simple life. Do you find a full calendar of social commitments enjoyable? I imagine one might become tired of the same people again and again."

"In different clothes, at different hours of the day." Raffles finished the thought. "It would be tedious if there weren't some fun in it," he admitted. "There's always some gossip to hear, or even a minor scandal. Romance, of course—in spring there are two or three weddings every week, and then by Christmas a slate of barely-secret infidelities. Politics. Crime."

Holmes' face lightened and his eyes sparked at the mention of his pet topic. "Ah, yes. Crime touches every class, and happens in every sort of place."

"Not a place like this, though," Raffles gently contradicted. He gestured widely at the peaceful path, the softly rustling tress, the tall grass at the lake's edge. When his hand came to settle, it lay over Holmes' long-fingered hand, resting in the crook of Raffles' arm.

Holmes said, "Even in a place like this. In fact, so very like this, it *is* this place."

Raffles widened his eyes. "What? Are you saying, Mr Holmes, that you know of a crime to have happened here in Sheepmeadow?"

"If one had not, I would not be here."

"Of course! Of course. You're a Londoner; why-ever would you be tucked up in this little dot on the map if not for the cause of solving a crime. Or perhaps preventing one?" Raffles ventured.

Obviously flattered, Holmes poured forth even more than Raffles might have hoped.

"More of an escort mission, I would say. There is a small parcel whose arrival I await—this very evening, on the late train, as a matter of fact—and which I must intercept, place for safekeeping, and then accompany back to civilization."

Raffles looked down at his fingers, stroking Holmes' own, and Holmes looked, too. After a breath's time, Raffles picked up the dropped thread of the conversation. "How very clandestine and intriguing," he said with quiet enthusiasm. "Might I inquire as to its contents?"

"Government documents," Holmes said dully.

Raffles did nothing to hide his disappointment, and said, "Oh."

"And rubies and diamonds," added Holmes, and he looked delighted when Raffles let go a little gasp and clutched his hand.

"Oh! My goodness, how exciting. And you are to guard them?" Raffles put on a concerned expression. "What, in your rooms there at the hotel? That hardly seems secure, even with the presence of your stout friend Dr Watson to watch over you."

"No, no. I have made arrangements to put them into a strong box."

"At the bank," Raffles said knowingly. "That's why you sent Watson and Bunny to see if they could spy it from the train!"

"I'm afraid I must confess that was a fool's errand, in order that you and I had a few moments alone together." Holmes looked to Raffles for approval of his ruse, which was quickly given, and Raffles graced him with a grateful smile.

"Where then, if not the bank?"

"In the post office, as a matter of fact," Holmes replied, looking pleased with himself. "Much less obvious, tidily secure. . .of every building in the village, it was the clear choice to house the parcel overnight. The postmaster assured me he will place it in his own, personal desk drawer."

"Leave it to the famous detective to suss out the best hiding spot for a cache of—diamonds, did you say? My goodness, that's exciting. My goodness."

"All in a day's work," Holmes demurred. They had come upon the little clearing with wooden benches and a view of the water framed by gold-leafed trees, and the two sat down together, very close as if needing protection from the air's autumnal chill.

"Or in a night's work," Raffles grinned. "You know, since you'll be leaving it overnight. Ah, what a ridiculous joke to make." He shook his head at himself, even though Holmes was looking at him with great warmth in his expression. "I confess I feel a bit stupid around you."

"You shouldn't, of course," Holmes assured him. Their hands were clasped together, and Holmes' long thumb brushed over Raffles' knuckle. "I think you're rather brilliant."

Raffles couldn't help but kiss him then, for Holmes was so sincere and after all, he'd just given Raffles—however unwittingly—exactly what he needed to get him and Bunny flush. Not that it was any hardship to kiss him. Holmes had some very good angles.

When they parted, Holmes grabbed onto Raffles' lapel and kept him close, resting their foreheads together. "Does it ever tire you?" he asked.

"All your high society living. Do you not ever want to stop and rest?"

Raffles had never considered the question. Rather than let himself think about it overmuch, though, he asked Holmes a similarly loaded question. "Well, what about you, burrowed down in Baker Street with only Dr Watson for your company. You must feel lonesome at times."

Satisfied that they were both equally exposed, and that neither would dare voice a reply without lying, Raffles ducked his head to claim another kiss —one which Holmes easily surrendered. There was something so comfortable in their embrace, and in the way their tongue-tips teased around each other, and in the soft sounds they made, that Raffles was unsettled by it. He broke away under the guise of needing to catch a breath, and even turned himself away just enough. After drawing a lungful of the fresh cool air, he reached for his cigarette case, placed two between his lips, and struck a match to light them. Passing one to Holmes, he gained his feet and walked a bit, not that there was anywhere to go, but he could pretend to admire the view.

"I think someday someone will come along and fall in love with you, Sherlock Holmes," Raffles mused. "The right one."

All sincerity, Holmes asked, "How will I know it's love, and that it's right?"

"I wish I knew," Raffles sighed. He brushed his

hand over the leathery leaves of a holly shrub, slick and prickly, and pulled a tiny berry free of its stem. "I'm no expert."

"Have you ever been in love, Mr Raffles?"

Raffles flicked ash from the end of his cigarette. "I can't say that I have—not truly. I'm too accustomed to my freedom to approach anything like domesticity, though a fleeting romance is a lovely thing, when it comes along." He looked penetratingly at Holmes, who smoked and stared at the horizon and did not meet Raffles' gaze. It would be a sweet thing indeed to fall in love with Sherlock Holmes, he thought, and despite his raptures at having been reunited with his dear friend Bunny, Raffles could not help but feel a pang of regret at the unlucky timing. Fleeting romance would have to suffice. He reminded himself it was all a confidence game, in the end, and that he should not be cruel.

Holmes dropped the butt end of his cigarette and turned the sole of his shoe upon it; Raffles used thumb and two fingers to let his fly, and it landed with a soft sizzle in the shallows of the lake's edge. Holmes rose and approached Raffles, but tangled his jacket on a branch as he came.

"Oh, blast," he cursed, "It's caught."

Raffles half-laughed and rushed to assist. Picking thorns from the threads of Holmes' coat, he finally freed him, though by then the jacket was half-off. "Shall I throw you in, now you're half-undressed?" Raffles joked, indicating the placid but surely very cold water before them. Holmes smiled, and Raffles helped him back into his sleeves, which ended in a further embrace, Raffles' hands beneath his jacket, stroking the satiny back of his waistcoat, feeling for his spine and the blades of his shoulders, at last settling at the sides of his waist. He kissed Holmes with heat, for he felt fired up with wanting him, and pulled him close, hard together at chest and thigh.

Against Raffles' lips, Holmes murmured, "Is this how it happens?"

Raffles pressed a last kiss on him, said nothing, felt his mouth and brows crumple helplessly. He almost shrugged his shoulders, and touched Holmes' hand, and walked away. Holmes followed.

Neither noticed the silent witness to their intimacies, the scarred man hidden in the woods, not near enough to hear, but near enough to see.

# Chapter Eight

Raffles had left Bunny thoroughly adored, muss-haired and naked sprawling across their too-small shared bed, asleep with parted lips, and taken himself outdoors to smoke and to walk. The moon was bright and full and high, perfectly matching Raffles' mood.

From halfway down the pavement, Raffles spotted the now-familiar silhouettes of Sherlock Holmes and Dr Watson just outside the entrance to the hotel where they had their rooms. Holmes was smoking a pipe, and Watson reeled about him in a manner stingingly familiar to Raffles' eye. He contemplated turning on his heel, but just then Watson must have caught sight of him, for he called out Raffles' name and waved him ahead. Raffles plodded toward them, dreading.

"Ah, Mr Raffles," Watson slurred, and as Raffles was by then close enough to endure it, the smell of drink off him was pronounced. "Barely recognised you without your loyal pup beside you." He barked a laugh at his own jibe.

Holmes said nothing; Raffles thought he might look embarrassed but there was a shadow across his narrow face that made true discernment impossible.

"Pleasant evening gentlemen," Raffles said, both greeting and parting at once.

"Won't you join us—me—for a whisky?" Holmes asked, and lay a hand on Raffles' arm. Watson gave a disapproving-sounding snort.

Raffles shook his head. "Thank you, no. There's been enough liquour consumed tonight, I think."

"Coffee, then?" Holmes prodded.

"Another time."

The disappointment was plain on Holmes' face, even as his friend Watson took him by the arm and pulled him close so they could fit side-by-side through the hotel's front door.

"Night, Raffles," Watson said over-loudly. "Say the same to that boy of yours."

When Raffles had rounded the block and returned to the rooming house, he entered the room without a care for whether Bunny was still asleep. He jiggled the key in the lock, let the crooked door fall hard shut, slouched on the edge of the bed, and threw his shoes at the floor. Bunny started a little, coming awake with a little gasp Raffles felt at the base of his skull.

"AJ...Are you quite all right?"

Raffles paced and huffed as he undressed. "Went for a walk and met Holmes and Watson on the pavement."

"Oh? Was there some kind of argument?" Bunny was up on his elbows, bare-chested with the bed covers up to his waist. His lips were softly swollen from sleep, his eyes dull and heavy.

"No. Watson was drunk. I had a friend once who overindulged and the smell off him was the same," Raffles muttered without thinking. Bunny's eyes widened and he raised his brows in questioning concern. Raffles was down to his shirtsleeves and began to unbutton his shirt. "I say friend but in truth he was an enemy I kept much too close. You, I know, are no fighter, Bunny. But that man forced me to learn, in order to defend myself against his drunken rages." It was all too much to tell; Raffles had never told it before, but once he'd opened the tap, he found he couldn't stop. "One late night, stumbling home from some ill-reputed venue or other, he fell and never again got up on his feet. I can't say I mourned his loss so much as felt relief because of it." He stooped to step out of his trousers, then slid into the bed beside Bunny, still in his small clothes. His feet were cold, and his hands were so cold they tingled. He opened his arm and Bunny tucked himself under it, stroking a hand over Raffles' chest in a very different way than he had before.

Raffles lowered his voice to a near-whisper. "In a strange way I have always felt a pang of guilt about it."

"The relief you felt?" Bunny murmured.

"That I could not persuade him to change his habits," Raffles contradicted him. "And the countless times I'd longed for an end to our acquaintance —whatever the means—as I did not have the fortitude to cut it off myself."

Bunny moved to look him in the eyes as he said, "No, AJ. Your wishes did nothing to speed your friend's bad end. Some men come to one, no matter the outward quality of their lives, nor the company they keep. Anyone would hate a friend who mistreated him so. I hate him, just hearing about it."

Raffles let himself smile the lightest bit, and leaned up to kiss Bunny's cheek. "You're kind," he said. After another kiss he asked, "Do you not think me monstrous?"

Bunny looked wounded. "I could never," he insisted, and shook his head to emphasise it.

"You are precious, Bunny," Raffles sighed. A look of bliss washed over Bunny's face, and he reached for the tiny buttons on Raffles' vest, began to work them open with nimble fingers. Raffles let his eyes fall closed.

After many kisses and caresses, Raffles had Bunny where he wanted him—in his arms, with his back against Raffles' chest, clutching each other's hands as he suckled and nipped at the hollow of

Bunny's shoulder, and beneath his ear where the edge of his jaw flexed each time he gasped. He was urgent against Bunny's backside, with his hand curled around Bunny's beautifully running prick. Both men let go base noises that only served to rile them more, make them both wilder. Raffles thought his heart would beat out of his chest, that he would never get back his breath, and when he spilled between the fleshy mounds of Bunny's rump, he groaned out every woe he'd ever held to make more space inside him for the pleasure of his lover's body against his own, the thick, silken cock in his hand. Bunny held off, wanting more, for longer, and Raffles scented a challenge, brought him along expertly, whispering filthy, romantic phrases into Bunny's funnily curled ear. When at last he could hold out no longer and came to his crisis, shuddering in Raffles' embrace, Bunny emanated frustrated surrender. Raffles felt triumphant, and kissed him all over his shoulders and neck, the edge of his jaw, until Bunny turned to him and they kissed away the last of their passion.

"You are precious, AJ," Bunny whispered, near-silent, just beside Raffles' ear.

Holmes had been very easily persuaded when

young Manders suggested the two pairs of London-
ers should claim a picnic luncheon from Button's
tavern and enjoy the sunshine, rather than pass the
day's finest hours indoors. Watson had protested;
Holmes suspected strongly that he was jealous of
Raffles. They two had spent a few long years with
each as the other's sole close companion. And now
Holmes was walking out in the village with Raffles,
while Watson had no such new acquaintance with
whom to pass the time.

Raffles told stories about cricket matches won
and nearly-lost (but in the end won), and Manders
put in enthusiastic comments about their days at
school. Holmes could not help but wonder if he had
been such a gnat-like pest to his senior, Raffles, even
then—and if so, how it was possible Raffles had tol-
erated his insistent, flighty company. The weather
was fine enough to remove their jackets and coats,
and the four sat in turned-back shirtsleeves on a
coarse wool picnic rug. Watson had removed his
shoes and socks and cuffed up his trousers to at-
tempt wading, but even his grit was not enough to
let him linger in the frigid water of the pristine lake.

"Do you hear that?" Manders piped up, lifting
his head and turning this way and that to catch
some noise or other. "It sounds like a cat."

"Probably nothing," Watson dismissed him.

Holmes, glad for a chance to perhaps be rid of
him, suggested, "It may be that you should go have

a look about; it sounds in terrible distress, and I wouldn't doubt there could be traps set at the edge of that farm." He motioned. "For foxes and the like."

Manders looked alarmed, and gained his feet. "I couldn't live with myself if I didn't at least have a look," he said, and appeared to be listening for a direction in which to go.

"Here, Bunny," Raffles said, and stood. "I'll go along with you."

Holmes' heart sank with disappointment. The two wandered around a bend, and out of sight. Holmes lay back on his elbows and planted his pipe between his teeth.

Watson chuckled. "I believe your heart is showing, Holmes," he marveled.

Holmes thought to deny it, but could find no reason, not to the one man in the world who knew him well enough to easily catch him in a lie. Instead, he sighed out, "I think I may love him, Watson."

Watson scoffed. "Sherlock Holmes—falling in love? There's no such animal."

In a thicket of trees, Raffles half-heartedly poked with a long branch at the grass and bushes along a narrow path, seeking Bunny's imaginary feline.

"Bunny, I think it would do for you to send letters to some of your acquaintances in society. Tell them you've had a holiday in the country, and that you simply can't wait to attend their balls and dinner parties as soon as you're back in town. Send notes to those fellows to whom you owe gambling debts; they'll assume you're coming back flush enough to repay them, or else wouldn't dare show your face."

Bunny frowned. "I thought we might stay longer," he said longingly. "We've got a decent room, and we're together..."

"No, we'll leave at the end of the week, as we planned," Raffles said crisply. "It's the best course."

"But—"

"We'll have our cash in hand soon, Bunny, and it's time we returned to the world."

"Well, I suppose if you say so, Raffles."

"I do say so. Ah, and here is your crying puss! Not in distress, after all, I'd say."

Raffles used his stick to hold aside some brush, and Bunny leaned down to look at a ginger-striped cat and five impossibly fresh kittens lined up at her belly. Bunny smiled. "Well, that's a relief!"

Supper that evening was lamb stew and roasted potatoes, and brick-hard bread to sop up the gravy.

Bunny and Raffles sat at a table in the dimmest corner, with a view of the fireplace as well as the door, and Raffles had carefully chosen his seat. In a small notebook, he had sketched a map of the village post office, and quietly told Bunny his plan to break in and fetch out the ruby-and-diamond treasure Holmes had told him about. Bunny maneuvered a mouthful in order to say around it, "You should tell Mr Holmes we're going back to London."

"What for?" Raffles demanded, looking irritated that Bunny had interrupted his work for discussion of leisure.

"Seems he'd like to know," Bunny said meaningfully. Though Raffles had proven the truth of his assertions that his intentions toward Holmes were all a stage play designed to lower Holmes' guard, Bunny could not but see the way Holmes looked at Raffles, and hear the change in his voice when he spoke to him. All of it was so familiar to him—echoing his own behaviour toward his dear friend—it put a pain in his heart on Holmes' behalf. He seemed a decent fellow, and Bunny did not wish to see him put through any unnecessary pain. "He may well miss you."

Raffles sighed, somewhere between exasperation and regret. After a moment he said, "He'll be back in London himself before long. Perhaps we'll meet again."

"Not if this plan ends in success," Bunny reminded, stabbing his fork in the air near the note-book's penciled map. "We'll be gone, and he'll be without the parcel he's here to fetch on behalf of Her Majesty. I doubt he'd want to see you again after that, except perhaps to do you harm."

Raffles shut the notebook and slipped it inside his jacket. He hummed through pursed lips. "You may be right," he admitted.

"I only know how I would feel, in his place."

"You're a better man than me, Bunny. And probably a better one than I deserve to call a friend."

Bunny defended himself as a rascal. "I told you I cheat at cards."

Raffles smiled at this, retrieving his notebook and scribbling a note in it. He tore out the page and folded it, motioned to a boy hanging about outside, looking for a coin or two. The boy came in, pulled off his cap.

"Can I help, sir?"

"Take this note to the hotel, for Mr Sherlock Holmes. No need to wait for a reply. There's a shilling, and another waits for you when you return."

"Thank you, sir! I'll be quick as a rabbit."

"Bit quicker, if you can," Raffles grinned, casting a glance in Bunny's direction. The boy ran off, and the two resumed their meal. It was only a moment or two, though, before a now-familiar figure of a man in an old military-issue coat, with a significant scar across his nose, came into the tavern and walked straight to their table.

"All lonesome, gents? Where's the detective?" he demanded.

"Sure, we dunno," Raffles said, in a voice not his own, which startled Bunny into staring speechlessness.

The man scowled, looming. "Me and mine got eyes on you," he said, "And we don't like people taking things ain't theirs. Leave it at that."

Raffles held his gaze—bravely, Bunny thought, for he had no wish to get into another fight while he still wore a fresh wound from the last one—and after a moment, the man turned and left. Bunny saw him looking up and down the street, clearly searching, before he stalked across it and vanished in shadow.

"That man's eyes are very strange," he said to Raffles. "What does he want with Mr Holmes, I wonder? I think it can be nothing good. He doesn't seem the type to need a mystery solved. More the type to cause a mystery to occur. Wouldn't you say, Raffles?"

Distracted, Raffles shook his shoulders as if awakening himself. "Hm? No. I mean, yes, he does seem the bad type. I've been able to run him off thus far, but we won't be here long. I'll remind Holmes to be careful of his back."

# Chapter Nine

Having received a handwritten, hand-delivered note from Raffles, Holmes waited outside the hotel, and Raffles appeared at the appointed stroke of the town's central clock. "I wonder if you'll walk with me," Raffles said, offering his arm. Holmes slipped his hand in and they strolled around the near corner, along the now familiar-to-them route to the lake. As the meagre gas lamps of the streets faded away behind them, they found their way by moonlight, eyes fixed on the ground to avoid anything over which they might stumble. They arrived at the clearing, assumed seats on a bench. Raffles used the motion of reaching for his cigarette case to settle himself at some small distance, and though Holmes longed for it, the men did not touch.

"It's been such a pleasure getting to know you," Raffles said. "You are, my dear fellow, so utterly novel. Your brilliance astonishes me."

Holmes felt his throat tighten around a curious lump, and clamped his pipe between his teeth.

Raffles offered his matchbox.

Raffles went on. "I could listen for hours to you, honestly, I could. Every time you speak, I learn more in a minute than I have in all my lifetime." In the dim light of evening, the water reflected glinting moonlight, and Holmes fixed his gaze on it rather than venture to look at Raffles. "But I know you well enough—even after our short acquaintance— to know that I am not the man you're waiting for."

Raffles took Holmes' hand and held it upon his knee, which was an act of tenderness Holmes found exquisitely painful. His pipe-smoke was bitter in his throat.

"Anything you might learn from me, though," Raffles said quietly, "You're certainly better off not knowing."

Holmes cleared his throat as he lifted his pipe from his mouth and held it away. "But ours is an unique sort of companionship, Raffles, and perhaps I could teach you something, as well."

In his peripheral vision, Holmes caught the motion of Raffles' soft shake of his head.

"I'm afraid there's nothing more to be said but good night." Raffles squeezed his hand all the tighter, and pressed a gentle kiss against Holmes' jaw. For fear he'd do something rash like beg him to reconsider, Holmes stayed still and silent. After a moment, Raffles released his hand and stood. "Good night, Sherlock Holmes," he said with some tenderness, and walked away into the darkness.

Holmes' pipe had gone out, and he felt his coat pockets only to realise he had pilfered Raffles' matches. As he drew one out to strike, there arose a rustling noise in the bushes just beyond his vision, and in a wild rush, he was gripped hard by the arms and dragged to his feet. He let go a shout, and kicked with all his might. The villain growled but did not release his hold, and the two struggled for control and balance. It was not like Holmes to be caught so thoroughly off-guard, and he cursed himself for it even as he attempted to wrench free.

There came the sound of thudding footsteps, running closer, and Raffles appeared. His balled fist crashed against the side of the scoundrel's face, knocking him sideways enough that Holmes was able to shake loose. Raffles went on throwing punches at the man on the ground, who scrabbled backward with dug-in heels, at last regaining his feet and turning to sprint. As he fled, he shouted back at Raffles, "You won't always be around, friend! You can't be!"

"Are you hurt?" Raffles asked, and took Holmes by the elbow to steady him. He panted, and his curly hair hung down across his brow until he swiped at it with his fingers.

"No," Holmes replied. "No. Only shaken."

"That fellow's doggedly persistent," Raffles commented with some amusement evident in his voice. "Come. I'll walk with you back to your rooms."

∞∞∞

Despite his best efforts to avoid meeting with Holmes again, it was nearly impossible for Raffles to keep himself away from anyone in such a small village, and the very morning after the violent encounter at the lake, he passed Holmes on the pavement near the tavern. They nodded to each other, but there was a sadness in Holmes' pale eyes Raffles could not ignore. He pulled him aside by a hand on his arm, and they stood close together at the opening of an alley. Once Raffles was sure they would not be overheard, he said, "If you have any heart left for me, meet me tonight at our spot by the water. Will you?"

Holmes did not hesitate. "Yes. Name the time and I shall be there waiting for you."

"Half past nine. I should be finished by then," he replied, without explanation of what he was to finish. "Promise you'll wait for me; I'll have something to give you."

Holmes nodded but said nothing. His gaze was penetrating; Raffles had to avert his own. Holmes touched his hand, and left him. As Raffles turned to walk away, Bunny appeared. Having poured out the story of the previous night's attack on Holmes, Raffles could see concern in Bunny's wide-open expression; he never hid a single thought or feeling that passed through him, and Raffles doubted he could if he wished to—which may go a way toward explaining why cheating at cards had never benefited him.

"He knows we're leaving tonight?" Bunny asked.

"What, 'we'? I've no need of you for the evening's sport, Bunny. Did you think you would accompany me?"

Bunny looked stricken, and though it made Raffles feel sick to see it, it was the desired effect of his sharp riposte. There was danger enough for them all—with the persistent, scarred stranger appearing around every corner, out of every shadow —and he wanted to remove at least one man he cared for from the risk of harm. Dr Watson looked the type who could handle himself in any kind of trouble, and Holmes had said he carried a pistol. Holmes himself was skilled in hand-to-hand fights, and in any event was not the sort to be manipulated to diversion from his plotted course. Hence it was his own young rabbit Raffles intended to chase away, to free himself from undue worry and to keep Bunny out of harm's way.

"Well, yes. I thought I could help," Bunny said haltingly.

Raffles scoffed a laugh. "I've been at my game for years without you, Bunny, and I'm sure to carry on without you for many more. Indeed, to have you hanging about is a distraction I am better off without."

"But. I could at least stay, to meet up after you've got—" Bunny remembered himself and lowered his voice. "After you've done the work. I'll wait for you in our room. There's no rush to get back to London once we're back in the black, not really. We can stay here until Mr Holmes and Dr Watson go, to keep an eye on them."

"What, and help them, too?" Raffles gruffed. "You do think rather much of yourself, Bunny. If ever I need your help, I'll whistle for you." He shook his head as he lit himself a cigarette. "You cannot even solve your own problems, but you appear to have mine all well and truly sorted."

Bunny looked forlorn and confused. Raffles settled his sick stomach with the smoke from his cigarette, and tried to trust his plan, to trust that Bunny would—once it was all explained—forgive him and welcome him back to his sweet embrace. All would be well, in the end, but for the time being. . . "I don't need you, Bunny my boy, any more than I need Sherlock Holmes on my arm. I think you should run along."

His face fallen and shoulders sagging, Bunny bit his lips shut, then said. "The last train this evening leaves Norwood at ten o'clock."

"Great news," Raffles said sternly. "You shall be on it."

Bunny nodded tightly. "If you think that's best," he said softly. "I'll do as you say. I hope to see you as soon as you come back to London. I'll wait for word from you." He did not sound hopeful.

"Yes, do. Lay low or you're likely to find yourself hanging by your thumbs out the window of a cards room." Raffles could hardly bear the sight of Bunny's face, his visage like that of a beaten dog with wide, disbelieving eyes. "Go on and pack your bag, then, rabbit. You don't want to miss that train."

# Chapter Ten

Trying to stay inconspicuous, dressed in Watson's borrowed coat and with his hat pulled down low on his brow, Holmes leaned against the wall of the post office with a newspaper held up in front of him. Footsteps approached, which he took for those of the postmaster, to whom he would entrust the parcel stowed away inside his waistcoat. When he looked up from his paper, though, it was AJ Raffles who appeared before him.

"Couldn't pass you by, once I'd noticed you," Raffles said softly, an admission of feeling that stung Holmes' heart.

"Watson tells me you and Mr Manders are leaving for London."

"What? Yes. Well. Bunny is, certainly. I have a few loose ends that need wrapping up."

"So is it tonight, then?" Holmes pressed. "After we meet at the lake?" He wondered if he was somehow being set up for something—sent to a place where he'd recently been near-kidnapped, by a man he really barely knew despite their affectionate exchanges, after dark, with promises of gifts—it was just the sort of thing he would certainly warn a client to beware of, should one bring him a similar scenario.

"I can't answer," said Raffles. "We'll have our moments together, though, regardless."

Holmes creased his newspaper for something to do with restless hands which badly wanted to grip and stroke Raffles, to hold him to the spot and prevent him leaving. "I wish to have more such moments," Holmes murmured. "More and more. But you seem not to want the same. And yet, here you stand."

"In my whole life, I have never belonged to anyone—until very recently, I never wanted to. It's a severely unsettling change." He looked around to be sure they were not watched, and lifted Holmes' hand to his lips, placing a kiss against his knuckles. "Tonight. Half past nine."

"Yes."

He walked away, and Holmes raised his paper in front of his face once more, and blinked his blurring eyes.

Bunny had already put his bag inside the cab, beneath its bench seat, and stood on the pavement, looking again and again at his wristwatch. For what reason he knew not, he still had hope that Raffles would appear and ask him to come back and help him, or get into the cab with him and come back to London. He looked down the pavement toward the rooming house and beyond it, the tavern, but Raffles did not come.

"Can't wait, if we're to make your train, sir," the driver said.

"Yes. All right."

Bunny made one more search, even standing on his toes, craning his neck. Finally, he climbed into the cab.

∞∞∞

In his sock feet and his darkest set of clothes, and with a black mask around his eyes, Raffles darted along, silent, in the shadows behind the post office. It would be an easy feat, he knew, so long as he kept it quick and kept himself out of sight. The rear door's single lock was easy enough to break, with only a screwdriver he'd borrowed from the rooming house's drunken landlord, under pretext of tightening the squeaking rails of the metal bed in his rented room. In a few seconds, his eyes adjusted to the darkness inside the building, and the door to the postmaster's office had no lock at all. Once he'd pushed it open, he waited, listening, crouched low just inside the door. Of course, there was nothing to hear for he was sure he had not been followed or in any other way observed.

He stole across the room and around the desk, backing the chair out from under it to access its drawers. Again he employed the screwdriver to open the lock on the bottom, righthand drawer, and slid it open. Behind a pile of papers tucked inside folders, he found what was wanted—a small, flat envelope just big enough for a set of folded documents and a great big handful of diamonds and rubies. His breath quickened with excitement as he drew it out; so enraptured was he with plans to buy Bunny a fine new suit of clothes and to squire him around to every supper club in London, both of them wearing diamond tie tacks, or perhaps he'd have a ring made, to slip on Bunny's pinky finger...

The parcel felt quite light in his hands, and he hastily, quietly, fingered it open. Inside, the documents Sherlock Holmes was meant to intercept, for some this-or-that matter of national security or scandal, Raffles neither knew nor cared. He lay the papers atop the desk and dipped his fingers back into the envelope, seeking the sharp, hard edges of already-cut stones.

There were none.

He turned the envelope upside down and shook it into his cupped palm. Nothing. His mind a blur of tragedy—no jewels, no money, and poor Bunny sent back to London owing debts to unsavoury characters!—he thrust a hand into the drawer once more, feeling for a second parcel, a box, a bag, anything at all, but came up empty. Either the jewels had never arrived in Sheepmeadow, or someone had beaten him to them.

Raffles collapsed back on his haunches, his spine against the wall and his head in his hand. It was a disaster he had never anticipated. Had Sherlock Holmes been lying to him about the gems, running on him a similar confidence game as he had tried to run on Holmes? But surely Holmes' emotion had been genuine; what reason would he have to lie?

He laughed cruelly at his own naivete. Lies upon lies had rolled off his very own tongue, and his emotion had appeared—had perhaps even been —genuine. Why should he be so surprised to have been had, by a notorious genius like Sherlock Holmes? He'd been a fool. Raffles wallowed another few moments in his despair, furious at the treachery of which he had surely been a victim. He recognised that to have been duped was no worse a fate than he deserved—he, a gentleman thief, who lived off the suffering of others. For the first time in his burgling career, he berated himself for his selfishness, and even worried for the state of his morals.

There was no time to waste, though, for he had

to get a message to Bunny, to return forthwith to the relative safety of their country burrow, lest he end up with a bashed-in head and a destroyed reputation.

Holmes waited on the bench, wanting desperately to smoke, but holding off. His hands were clenched as if in angry prayer, his knuckles white with the effort, and pressed against his lips. He got to his feet and paced; the grass beneath his feet reflected frosty-white in the moonlight.

"Thought you'd be smarter than to show up 'ere again," came a rocky voice, from somewhere too close for comfort. "And all alone, no less."

Raffles returned to his rented room, quickly changed into more suitable clothes, and was back on the pavement by a quarter past nine. He walked a route to take him past Holmes' hotel, just in case he might intercept him on his way to the lake, but did not encounter him, and so walked on around the corner and up the road. The folded documents were inside his jacket; he'd hand them over to Holmes with best wishes for a long and happy life, and bid him one last goodbye.

As Raffles came into the clearing, his eyes immediately fell on the wooden benches, looking for Holmes, but both stood empty. His gaze drifted across the open space until it stopped upon a crumpled, shadowy figure on the ground. At once he recognised the tartan pattern of Holmes' Inverness coat. He sucked in air and ran to him.

"My god! Holmes!" he knelt beside the prostrate man and felt for his shoulders, pulled him up by his lapels to settle across Raffles' lap. "Holmes! Say you are all right!"

"He came for the papers. That's all he wanted, in the end," Holmes said weakly, his mouth crooked with a slight, ironic smile. "If only he had asked in a civil manner, I might even have given them up. If I'd had them." His voice hitched, and although it was a difficult judgement to make in the low light of the moon and stars, Raffles thought his face looked pale.

"What has he done? Are you hurt?" Raffles demanded, running hands over his friend's arms and inside the front of his coat. His shirt was thickly soaked; Raffles gasped and pulled his hand away from the awful sensation just as the hot, coppery reek of blood found his nostrils. "He's cut you? God in heaven!"

Holmes gripped him hard by the arm. "Inside

my jacket. Look in my pocket." He grimaced with obvious pain. Raffles, in a stunned horror, did as he was told, slipping his clean hand into Holmes' jacket. There was an unmistakable velvet bag inside, small enough to grip in his fist. When he did so, he felt the gravelly grind of well-cut stones, not a few. "I wanted you to have them," Holmes murmured. "I have no use for them, and Her Majesty can do without."

His voice trailed to near-nothing; Raffles tried to gather him closer. Help was so far away, and Raffles could not leave him.

"Did you see?" Holmes whispered, his eyes closed. "I found a green carnation for my buttonhole."

"Oh, Holmes," Raffles sobbed. "Only hold on. We'll get you well in no time. Can you stand? You can lean on me." It felt horribly futile but desperation made him babble. "Holmes, I'm sorry. Do you hear? I'm sorry I was disingenuous; I had no idea you would be so prone to sentiment. So deeply, and so soon—*oh, god!*—I only meant it as a game. I see now how cruel I was, and I beg you—*beg you*—to forgive me."

He pressed his lips against Holmes' closed eye and found the thin skin there worryingly cool.

Raffles did not notice a pair of lovers happening upon the scene of Sherlock Holmes—insensate on the ground—and AJ Raffles knelt beside him with a gory coating of blood all up one arm. He stayed there with Holmes, in the moonlight, helpless, until at last came a commotion of police, led along by the lovers who had found them. Raffles went silently, hanging his sorry head, without a fight.

"Alive...Holmes is alive."

Raffles repeated the words again and again, trying to believe them though he could barely comprehend their meaning; Holmes had been so pale and slack in his arms. A hard-looking policeman called Lestrade sat across from him, smoking and drinking coffee. "There's going to be a shocking amount of trouble," Lestrade commented. "Once word gets out Sherlock Holmes has been so grievously attacked—nearly murdered!—hammers are going to fall."

"I held him in my arms. He wept," Raffles muttered, aloud but to himself. "Imagine. A man like that, one man in a million, weeping over—" He caught himself, cut himself off. All at once he was choking.

Another policeman, this one with a pronounced Scots accent, strode into the little room at the back of the police station. "There'll be a vigilante mob," he pronounced dourly. "Rumours are rampant that the detective's been killed, and there's no convincing anyone otherwise, now the surgeon's rushed with him back to London."

"He wore a green carnation," Raffles said. "I didn't even notice."

A third policeman, this one clearly junior, arrived to report he'd found nothing of value at the scene of the crime. Lestrade rubbed his temple, indicating an immediate and forceful headache had overtaken him, and told the Scotsman, MacKenzie, "I can't get anything from this one. Put him in a cell."

Bunny's cab stopped suddenly; a crowd was gathered and its agitation stirred the air. The driver leaned down to ask a man passing what the noise was all about.

"Did you not hear?" the man cried. "That detective, the famous one from London—Sherlock Holmes—was killed!"

Bunny hammered on the roof the cab and yelled, "Take me back!"

Raffles hunkered down lowly on a rough wood bench in one of two jail cells. The station door banged open and in rushed Dr Watson, brandishing a pistol and shouting. "Bring him out! Bring out the filthy mongrel at once!"

A gang of furious townsfolk rushed in behind him and surged past, manhandling the policemen and shoving them into the empty cell. One man locked it while another worked to unlock the one that secured Raffles.

"I'll beat you until you cannot stand," Watson howled. "Then hand you over to whomever else shall want to end you, though none wish it so profoundly as I do." Three men put hands on Raffles and wrestled him out of the cell. Watson's face was so twisted with fury he barely looked like a man. Raffles, still too stunned to believe Holmes had survived after what he had witnessed of the man's suffering, did not resist.

Bunny's heart was in his throat; Holmes, dead? He knew he must get back to Raffles at once, for fear something must have gone terribly wrong with Raffles' plan. And what of that scarred man who had been hanging about endlessly the whole time they'd been in Sheepmeadow, pestering Sherlock Holmes at every turn? He once more pounded his fist impatiently against the cab's ceiling, calling for the driver to make haste.

"I would never have hurt him, he was a friend," Raffles pleaded. Men held him upright by both arms, there in the alley beside the police station. Others took their turns throwing punches at his face and belly, once in the middle of his chest.

Watson's voice was gravelly with anger and a barely-controlled agony Raffles recognised. "You said you didn't need him," he ranted. "I heard you myself, outside the hotel with Manders. Why did you kill my dearest friend?"

Raffles' head spun and he could not entirely trust his vision. But he felt sure he recognised one laughing face in the crowd as that of the man who had accosted Holmes again and again—the man with the jagged scar across his face. Before he could speak, another blow crashed against his jaw, and he spat blood. Surely he would be beaten to death.

Outside the police station, Bunny barely let the cab stop before he threw open the door and leapt down to the pavement, rushing toward a commotion of men in the alley.

"Let me through!" he bellowed, and shoved his way past shoulders and elbows, until he saw Raffles caught in the arms of two angry men, looking hazily off into the gathered mob. Amid the gang, with a perturbing grin on his rough-hewn face, stood the scarred man.

Raffles swallowed hard and addressed him. "You?" he shouted. "It was you! It must have been!" Ignoring his exclamation, the men went on beating and kicking Raffles, who hung limp in the arms of those employed to hold him steady for the assault.

Desperate and blind with panic, Bunny took three hard strides and jumped at the scarred man, knocking him off his feet and then wrestling to keep him on the ground. "I wouldn't have touched him if he'd come across with what I wanted," the man spat. "I'd never have done it if he'd just kept quiet."

The cab driver rushed forward carrying the ring of keys used to lock the cells; behind him came the policemen who had been jailed by the mob. Bunny, kneeling on the scarred man's chest, though he struggled with all his might to throw Bunny off him —saw Raffles lying unmoving and senseless upon the ground, and turned to the policemen.

"He's the one!" he shouted, indicating the man beneath him. "You've made a mistake!"

The crowd around Raffles had quieted, and their faces showed they doubted their harsh judgement of the situation. The police moved in to seize the scarred man, and Bunny rushed to Raffles' side. He ducked down close to his face, listening for breath, which burbled around the blood in Raffles' mouth and nose.

"AJ," he said, and touched Raffles' face. "AJ, wake up."

Later, Raffles was attended by the absent doctor's junior, who gave him pain relief and bandaged his wounds, instructed him not to ignore any pain in his belly but otherwise all that was required was time to rest and mend. Bunny was by his side; the two sat in hard wood chairs across from Lestrade's desk. It had taken hours to sort out the mess and clear Raffles' name. The scarred man refused to confess to the vicious assault; rather, he had been vouched for by a man of some repute in London, and so was released and ordered back to the city, and to not so much as turn around to look back at Sheepmeadow or else suffer the consequences.

Bunny was writing out a note to send ahead of

them, to the valet at the Albany, asking that Raffles' rooms be made ready for his return from his country holiday. Raffles wondered, "What will happen to Watson—brandishing that pistol and sending a crazy mob to try to murder me?"

Lestrade nodded and said firmly, "He'll get what he deserves."

"He believed he had lost Sherlock Holmes," Raffles mused. "Perhaps keep that in mind, and tread lightly." Lestrade looked thoughtful but did not commit to a reply. Raffles cast a glance toward his friend, busy with his letter, and addressed Lestrade once more. "Please tell Mr Manders I'll be back."

The cold was bone-deep, and the water churned blackly beneath the cloud-shrouded moon. Raffles found a few pebbles and walked up to the lake's edge. He tossed them in, thinking of how Holmes had said the rings they made were eloquent, reminders of the rippling consequences of human action. He slipped a hand into his coat pocket and curled it around the velvet bag. He'd keep one—the best, prettiest one—and have it made into a tie tack or a ring he, himself, would wear in honour of Sherlock Holmes, a fine man whom he had for a little while loved.

Footsteps crackled, and a comfortingly familiar voice accompanied it. "Raffles?" Bunny arrived at his side, and the two eased into a grateful embrace. Raffles held him hard, wanting to apologise for having sent him away, thank him for saving him from the mob, make him know that in the end, Bunny was the only friend he wanted—wanted him for life.

"Come on, Raffles," Bunny murmured between kisses. "It's time we go home."

# About The Author

## Penny Doyle Douglas

Penny Doyle Douglas lives and writes near Boston. The Ides is her third novel.

# Books By This Author

**At Night In The Floating World**

**North Hope Cove**